W9-CTT-167

FIRST KISS

Nikki dialed Haley's number. Just to see how things went, she told herself. Haley answered on the first ring.

"Hi, Haley," Nikki said, trying to sound casual. "How was the movie?"

"Incredible!" Haley said. "Alex is so sweet. And romantic! Why didn't you tell me how great he was? I think he might just be perfect."

"I'm not sure I'd go that far," Nikki replied.

"No? Listen to this," Haley said. "When we got home, he came inside with me for a minute. We were standing there, talking about practice tomorrow, and then he took both my hands in his and kind of held them for a minute. And then . . ." Haley paused.

"What?" Nikki held her breath. She wasn't sure she wanted to hear the answer.

"He kissed me! My first real kiss. It was fantastic. It was—"

Nikki interrupted her. "That's great, Haley. I'm really happy for you. But I've got to go now. I'll call you tomorrow, okay?"

She hung up before Haley could say another word. There was a sick feeling in her stomach. And somehow she knew it was only going to get worse.

MORE
THAN
FRIENDS

Melissa Lowell

Created by Parachute Press

A SKYLARK BOOK

NEW YORK • TORONTO • LONDON • SYDNEY • AUCKLAND

With special thanks to Darlene Parent, director of
Sky Rink Skating School, New York City

RL 5.2, 009–012

MORE THAN FRIENDS
A Skylark Book / November 1996

ISBN 0-553-48499-0

Published simultaneously in the United States and Canada

PRINTED IN THE UNITED STATES OF AMERICA

OPM   0 9 8 7 6 5 4 3 2 1

1

Beautiful, Nikki Simon thought. This is great!

Nikki moved smoothly into her backward crossovers. She stroked her way across the ice, building momentum. Out of the corner of her eye she could see her partner, Alex Beekman, as he skated next to her. Nikki moved slightly ahead of him and pulled herself down into a sit spin. Beside her, Alex did the same. Nikki sensed, rather than saw, that they were perfectly synchronized. They finished the spin that ended their routine and held their final pose with their arms flung high over their heads.

"Not bad," Kathy called to them. She stood to one side of the rink, near the boards.

Nikki flashed a grin at Alex. Coming from their coach, Kathy Bart, "not bad" was high praise. Kathy's nickname was Sarge, and sometimes she really acted like a tough army sergeant!

Kathy was hard to please. She had nearly made it to the top as a skater. Several years earlier she'd placed fourth in the Nationals, just missing a chance to go to the Olympics. Kathy was demanding, but she was also a terrific coach.

"Kathy seems happy," Alex murmured to Nikki.

"Yeah. We must look good," Nikki whispered back. They skated over to Kathy and stopped with a spray of ice.

"If you two keep this up, you're going to be in great shape for the Ice Theater show," Kathy said. "But you've got only two weeks to master that throw double axel. It's still shaky."

"We'll get it," Nikki told Kathy. "Don't worry."

"Just practice it tomorrow morning," Kathy said.

"Okay." Nikki and Alex spoke in unison. Nikki burst out laughing. They were still perfectly synchronized!

"And Alex," Kathy added, "keep working with Ernie in the weight room. The stronger you get, the easier it'll be to give Nikki the height she needs."

"I know," Alex answered. "I'm on the case."

"Good. I'll see you both in the morning."

Nikki and Alex bent to put on their skate guards.

"We keep getting better all the time," Alex boasted. "We're practically as good as Karen Morris and Michael Gilbert."

Nikki laughed. "Not quite," she replied. Morris and Gilbert were Nikki's absolute favorite pairs skaters. In fact, they were starring in the big show at the Ice Theater of Philadelphia.

"I still can't believe we were chosen to perform with them," Nikki told Alex. "I feel like we just won the lottery or something. We are so lucky!"

"Hey, it was more than luck," Alex reminded her.

"True," Nikki replied.

She and Alex were only one of many pairs from the area who had submitted tapes of their routines to the organizers of the Ice Theater show. It helped that Nikki and Alex were members of Silver Blades. It was one of the top skating clubs in the country. And Nikki and Alex were one of the better pairs in the club.

Still, they had been competing against other talented skaters for a spot in the show, including Nikki's good friend Haley Arthur and her partner, Patrick McGuire. They belonged to Silver Blades, too, and they were good—really good.

"But it *is* lucky that our new routine is to *Grease,*" Nikki said to Alex. "I mean, the ice show is called *Broadway on Ice.*"

"So?" Alex asked.

"So *Grease* was a hit musical on Broadway," Nikki explained. "Maybe the show's producers liked the idea that we don't need to learn a whole new routine before the show."

"Yeah." Alex shrugged. "Of course, the tape we sent them just happened to be totally fantastic."

"Yeah," Nikki agreed. "We really worked hard the last few months. I guess it paid off."

"Big-time!" Alex grinned and tugged the end of Nikki's long braid. "All we need now is a perfect throw double axel."

"We'll do it," Nikki said. She turned toward the women's locker room. Alex was already disappearing into the men's locker room. He gave her a little wave.

"See you later," Nikki called. "And try to be early, okay?"

Alex nodded as the door closed behind him. Nikki frowned. She wasn't sure Alex had heard her. Maybe I should remind him about our plans for this evening, she thought.

But Alex was already gone. Never mind, Nikki told herself. He won't forget.

They were going to watch a tape she'd made the month before—of *Hot Rocks on Ice*. It was the best TV figure-skating show Nikki had ever seen. She couldn't wait to see it again with Alex. She had even baked them a batch of pecan brownies to munch as they watched. The pecan brownies were Alex's favorites. Nikki smiled. She and Alex weren't only partners, they were close friends, too. They had a special relationship, on the ice and off.

Nikki pushed through the door into the women's locker room. A stream of excited chatter greeted her. All her close friends were already inside. Tori Carsen, Haley Arthur, Amber Armstrong, and Martina Nemo were grouped around a bench, changing into street clothes.

Nikki grinned at the outfit Haley wore. It was pure

Haley: an oversized long-sleeved T-shirt that had a huge picture of her favorite rock band, torn jeans, and heavy boots. A silver earring shaped like a giraffe dangled from one ear.

"Hi, Nikki!" Amber called. "You and Alex looked awesome today. You were almost as good as Gilbert and Morris."

Nikki grinned. Amber was only eleven, but she was one of the most talented singles skaters in Silver Blades.

"Thanks," Nikki told her.

"Anyway, it all sounds great," Tori remarked to someone, continuing her conversation. She shook out her long blond hair and brushed it vigorously. Tori was fourteen. She was the other top singles skater in the club. Tori slipped into a pair of blue suede ankle-high boots that matched her blue leggings and oversized sweater.

Tori's mom was a fashion designer. She made all Tori's skating clothes. But even Tori's everyday outfits were gorgeous.

"So where are you guys going?" Tori asked.

Where is *who* going? Nikki wondered. She sat on the bench near Haley and untied her skates.

"I don't know," Haley answered. "To the movies, or maybe to the mall."

"Who cares?" Martina teased. Martina was fifteen. She had long, glossy black hair and beautiful dark eyes. She also skated singles. She was talented, though not nearly as good technically as Tori or Amber. "Haley doesn't care where they go," Martina added.

"You're right," Haley agreed. "Anywhere is fine with me, as long as it's with *him*." Haley's eyes glowed with excitement.

"Him?" Nikki echoed. She stared at Haley.

"Whoa. This sounds like true love—with a capital *T* and a capital *L*," Martina said.

"Haley's in love!" Amber added in a singsong.

Haley's face turned nearly as red as her hair, but she didn't answer.

"Wait a minute." Nikki stared at Haley. "What's this all about? You're in love and I don't even know about it?"

"Not in love," Haley said, but she was still blushing. "I just have a date with Alex. I ran into him at the park yesterday. We were both in-line skating, and we ended up spending the afternoon together. And then he asked me out."

"On a date? For real?" Nikki asked.

"Yup." Haley beamed. "He's coming over tonight, and we're—"

"Tonight?" Nikki interrupted. "But Alex is coming over to my house tonight," she said. "We're going to watch a video. We made plans last week."

Haley shrugged. "He must have forgotten. I mean, the date was his idea, not mine." She closed her eyes and smiled dreamily. "Isn't it great?"

Martina nudged Tori with her elbow. "Yeah. True love," she teased. "It's written all over her face."

Nikki pulled her green sweater over her black turtleneck. She couldn't help feeling a little irritated. "Well, couldn't you talk to Alex? Change the date to another night or something?"

"Are you crazy?" Haley gaped at her. "You know how long I've been waiting to go out with Alex. Like, since the Junior Nationals. He asked me out then, remember? But we couldn't go."

Haley's parents had just separated. Her dad was living in Canada. At first Haley had thought she wanted to move there with him. But she had soon realized she was better off at home in Seneca Hills with her mom and her sister, Morgan.

When it happened, Haley had been very upset about the separation—too upset to think about dating. But she was used to the new arrangement now.

Haley stuffed her skating things into her backpack. "No way I'm changing this date," she repeated to Nikki. "You guys always watch tapes together. This is special," she insisted.

"But Haley, it's Monday," Nikki protested. "You have practice tomorrow morning. Alex has practice tomorrow morning. Remember? Five-forty-five A.M.?"

"Lighten up, Nikki," Tori chimed in. "You sound like my mother!"

"Besides, it's winter vacation," Martina reminded her. "No homework tonight, no school tomorrow. Haley can sleep the rest of the day if she wants."

"Anyway, we're not going to stay out late," Haley added. "Though I wouldn't mind missing a little sleep for Alex." She lowered her voice a little. "I really do like him. And I want to find out if he really likes me."

"Well, it sounds like bad timing to me." Nikki yanked her sneakers on and started to lace them up. "We've got a big show coming up."

"Alex doesn't seem too worried," Haley pointed out. "Anyway, that's the good thing about going out with another skater. Alex and I both understand about practices."

Nikki raised her eyebrows. "That didn't help me much with Kyle," she said. Kyle Dorset was tall, with blue eyes and long brown hair. He was cute but painfully shy. He and Nikki used to go out about once a week. Used to, Nikki thought sadly.

"Oh, Kyle doesn't count. He's a hockey player," Haley said.

Nikki put her hands on her hips. "So? He still has to get up really early and spend a lot of time at the rink. And that made it harder for us to get together, not easier."

Tori broke in. "Are you saying that because you and Kyle broke up, Haley shouldn't go out with Alex? That makes no sense, Nikki."

"That's not what I'm saying!" Nikki's exasperation was growing by the minute. "Besides, Kyle and I didn't really break up. We just hardly go out anymore." Nikki undid her braid. She began brushing her hair with short, firm strokes. "I just think it's hard to be serious about a guy and serious about skating, too."

She turned to Haley. "So I don't think you should make a big deal out of this date."

"I'm not making a big deal out of it," Haley said. "You are."

"Yeah, well, you know Alex," Nikki began.

"What does that mean?" Haley asked. Tori and Martina turned to stare at Nikki.

Nikki hesitated. "Well, he's such a flirt," she said. Haley glared at her. "Oh, forget it," Nikki finished.

Haley zipped up her backpack. She looked Nikki straight in the eye. "I'm not going to remind Alex he's got plans with you tonight. And I hope you won't, either."

Nikki held Haley's gaze for a moment, then shrugged and looked away. "I won't say anything else about it," she promised.

Haley slung her jacket over one arm and picked up her skate bag and backpack. "I'll see you guys later." She walked to the door and pushed it open. "Wish me luck tonight."

"Good luck," Martina and Tori said together.

Nikki hesitated. "Have fun," she finally said. But Haley had already gone out the door.

2

If only vacation could last forever! Nikki thought. She dug a handful of popcorn out of the bowl and crammed it into her mouth. She stretched out on the family room couch and flipped through the latest issue of *Skating* magazine. It felt great to be home from afternoon practice without any homework to worry about.

The phone rang. Nikki jumped up to answer it, almost spilling her popcorn. She grabbed the phone. "Hello?"

"Hey, Nikki," Alex said. "How's my favorite partner?"

"Hungry. Stuffing my face with popcorn." Nikki popped a few more kernels into her mouth.

"So what else is new?" Alex laughed. "I can't believe you can eat so much and stay so thin."

"What can I say?" Nikki chuckled. "It's a gift."

"Well, don't get carried away," Alex teased. "Remember—every pound you gain, I have to lift."

"I know, I know," Nikki teased back. She scraped up more popcorn and tossed it into her mouth. "Practice went great this afternoon. What did you think?" she asked.

"Yeah, not bad. We'll get there." Alex paused. "Did Haley see us?"

"I don't think so. Why?"

"Well, she might have some suggestions," Alex replied. "You know, like when she helped us learn the death spiral."

Nikki shrugged. "But Haley and Patrick can't even do a throw double axel yet. How's she supposed to know what we're doing wrong?"

"Oh, I don't know . . . I just think Haley's real sharp. She'd make a good coach, don't you think?"

Nikki twisted the phone cord around her finger. "Yeah, well, we've got a coach already, remember? And Kathy thinks we're doing fine."

"We are. I just wondered . . . did Haley tell you she and I are going to the mall tonight?"

"Yeah, she mentioned it. But you—" Nikki stopped herself. She wanted to remind Alex that he was supposed to come over to her house that night. But Haley would be furious.

"Well, I'll ask her about the throw double axel then," Alex said. "I'll let you know what she thinks."

"Uh, Alex," Nikki began, "are you really nervous about the show?"

"Not really," Alex said. "Why?"

"Well, why else would you think we need so much help?" Nikki asked. "Especially from Haley. I mean, she's a good pairs skater, but she's really no better than you and me. Anyway," Nikki went on, trying to change the subject, "I'm trying not to be nervous about the show. But sometimes when I think about it, I break out in a cold sweat."

"Relax," Alex said. "It's going to be a piece of cake. You know, Haley thinks we should wear the dark green outfits for it."

Nikki frowned. "Kathy doesn't think so. She said I should wear my bright pink dress and you should wear your black pants and black shirt. I mean, we're supposed to be in *Grease*. The green outfits wouldn't look right." Nikki took a deep breath. "I thought we'd already agreed on that," she added.

"It's just that Haley thinks the green dress brings out your green eyes," Alex said.

"Alex, no one in the audience will see my eyes," Nikki said, totally exasperated. "And since when is Haley such a fashion expert? She'd skate in torn jeans and an old sweatshirt if Kathy let her."

"Hey, I like the way Haley dresses," Alex protested.

Nikki rolled her eyes, even though Alex couldn't see her. "I like the way she dresses, too. But I don't think she's the best person to decide what we wear in the show."

"Okay, okay," Alex said. "Just think about it, all right?"

"I—hold on a second," Nikki said as her mother came in from the kitchen. She was carrying Nikki's baby brother, Benjamin.

"Nikki, could you take Ben for a while?" her mom asked. "I'm trying to get dinner going, and he won't let me put him down. I can't cook with a baby on my hip." Mrs. Simon tried to hand Ben over to Nikki, but he clung to his mother, burying his head against her shoulder.

Nikki tucked the phone between her ear and shoulder and reached for Ben. He started to whimper, but then he caught sight of the telephone cord. He snatched the phone from Nikki and promptly dropped it on the carpet.

"Benny, cut it out!" Nikki scooped the phone up. "Sorry about that, Alex. I've got to go. My mom needs me to take Ben."

"Okay. But I need to ask you something else," Alex replied. "Call me back later, okay?"

"Okay. Bye." Nikki barely managed to get the words out before Ben grabbed the phone again. He shoved the receiver into his mouth and chewed on it with his brand-new teeth.

"You doofus," Nikki said fondly. "Telephones are not for eating." She took the phone away.

Ben started to howl, but Nikki grabbed a toy truck from the basket of toys on the floor. "Look, Benny," she said. She pushed the truck back and forth across the carpet. Ben reached for the truck and put it in his mouth.

Nikki chuckled. Ben was so sweet! It was hard to believe there had ever been a time when she didn't want a baby brother. Ben was only ten months old, but she could barely remember what it had been like when he wasn't around.

Nikki picked the baby up. "Come on, Benny boy," she said. "I'll build you a block tower, and you can knock it down."

"There. That's done." Mr. Simon rinsed the last saucepan and turned it upside down in the dish drainer. Nikki wiped down Benjamin's high-chair tray. "Thanks for your help, sweetie," her dad said.

"No problem." Nikki scraped the last of a blob of applesauce off the tray and tossed the sponge in the sink.

"And now, since you're such a helpful, hardworking, and all-around super kid, your mother and I have a surprise for you," Mr. Simon announced.

"A surprise? Like fudge sundaes or something?" Nikki's eyes gleamed.

"Are you kidding? And spoil that nice low-fat dinner your mom made?" Mr. Simon patted his stomach. He was always on a diet of some sort. "Besides," he added, "didn't you just polish off two of those brownies you made?"

"Yeah," Nikki said. "So what's your point?"

Mr. Simon laughed. "My point is, I think that's enough sweets for tonight. Anyway, we've got something better planned."

Now Nikki was really curious. "What?"

"If I told you, it wouldn't be a surprise," he teased. "Run upstairs and tell your mom we're ready to go, okay?"

"Okay." Maybe it was a good thing Alex wasn't coming over after all, Nikki thought.

A few minutes later they were all in the car. Mr. Simon pulled out of the driveway and onto the street. "Well, we're obviously not going to the mall," Nikki said. "You went the wrong way."

"Good thinking," Mr. Simon said. "Not the mall. There aren't any good surprises there, anyway."

"Oh, I don't know," Nikki answered. "Clothes, video games, jewelry, books . . ."

"It's not that kind of surprise," Mrs. Simon said. "Not a buying-something surprise."

"And not an eating-something surprise," Nikki said.

"That's right," Mr. Simon said. "Besides, you're thinking small. This is a big surprise."

Nikki was mystified. "A big surprise?" she asked. Neither of her parents answered. Her mother reached into the backseat and patted Ben's foot. He was already fast asleep in his car seat. Nothing knocked him out faster than riding in the car.

Her dad turned onto the highway, following a sign that pointed to the airport. Nikki sat up straighter.

"You're going to the airport to pick up tickets to some-place," she guessed. Her face lit up. "Disney World?"

Her mother laughed. "Not that big a surprise."

Nikki thought for a moment. "Gran's coming to visit?" She leaned forward, straining against the seat belt.

"No," her dad said. "But you're getting warmer. Much warmer."

"Aunt Jean?" Nikki guessed. "It would be great if Aunt Jean could see me in the Ice Theater show." Jean was her dad's sister and Nikki's favorite relative.

"My lips are sealed," her father said.

"And stop guessing. You'll ruin the surprise," her mother added.

They soon arrived at the airport, parked the car, and headed for the terminal. Nikki followed her mom and dad through the lobby and toward the arrival gates. He finally stopped in front of one gate. Nikki read the sign, which said the arriving flight was from Missouri. They could see the plane on the runway. As the pas-sengers streamed off, Nikki gazed from one to an-other.

She frowned. The surprise had to be a visit from some relative. Her family had moved to Pennsylvania from Missouri, and her mom was always complaining about not seeing relatives from home often enough.

"Come on, Dad, stop teasing," Nikki complained. "It must be Gran or Aunt Jean. Or maybe Uncle—"

Nikki stopped talking. A slender girl in jeans walked

quickly toward them. She wore a pink sweatshirt that had an enormous white teddy bear printed on the front.

"That sweatshirt . . . ," Nikki murmured. Her eyes rose to the girl's face. "No! It can't be!"

3

"Erica!" Nikki screamed.

Erica threw her arms around Nikki. Nikki hugged her hard in return.

"I can't believe it." Nikki stepped back and stared. Erica Summers was her best friend from Missouri. They hadn't seen each other in almost two years.

"Why didn't you tell me you were coming?" Nikki demanded.

"I didn't even know until last night," Erica replied. "Your mom and my mom made all the plans. Neat, huh?"

Nikki grinned. "Yeah."

"Come on, girls," Mr. Simon said. "Let's go get Erica's luggage."

"I've got it," Erica said. "This is it." She pointed to the backpack on her back.

"That's all you've got?" Nikki asked. "How long are you staying?"

"For a week—until next Tuesday."

Nikki looked at the backpack doubtfully. There couldn't possibly be enough clothing in there for a whole week.

"Hey, Nikki, do you remember this?" Erica pointed to her sweatshirt. "Do you still have yours?"

Nikki hesitated. "I, um, I'm not sure," she said. She and Erica had bought the matching sweatshirts when Nikki still lived in Missouri. But that had been a couple of years before. Nikki wouldn't be caught dead in the sweatshirt now. It was so babyish. She couldn't tell Erica that, though.

"I think it shrank or something," Nikki said.

Ben woke up and sleepily rubbed his eyes. "Hey there, Ben," Erica said. She touched his hand gently, and he grabbed her finger. "Boy, you're cuter than the photos Nikki sent me!"

"Okay, girls, let's head home," Mr. Simon said. He lifted Erica's backpack off her shoulders and slung it over one of his own. "It's getting close to Ben's bedtime."

"Not that he'll go to sleep," Mrs. Simon said. "After the little nap he just had, he'll probably be up until midnight."

"I'll stay up with him," Erica volunteered. "I love babies."

"Hey." Nikki poked Erica. "Who'd you come to visit, me or Ben?"

"Well," Erica said, "now that you mention it . . ." She grinned and then hooked her arm through Nikki's. "You, of course. This is going to be great."

An hour later they were up in Nikki's room. Nikki couldn't get over the surprise. It was going to be great having Erica stay all week! Nikki opened a dresser drawer, took out a stack of sweaters and T-shirts, and crammed them into another drawer. "There," she told Erica. "Now you've got someplace to put your stuff."

Erica opened her backpack and took out two sweatshirts, a pair of jeans, and some underwear.

"That's it?" Nikki said. "That's all you brought?"

"Yeah, sure." Erica tossed the clothes into the drawer. "I figured we wouldn't go anyplace fancy. That's all I need for just hanging around."

Nikki smiled. "You haven't changed a bit."

"Yes, I have. I'm an inch taller." Erica drew herself up to her full height. "See?"

"No, I mean the clothes," Nikki said. "You were never too interested in them."

"Oh, that." Erica shrugged. "Yeah, you're right. Too much trouble."

"And your hair is the same."

Erica stroked her brown ponytail and posed as if she were a famous movie star. "Well, this look, it's me, you know?"

"It sure is." Nikki giggled. Erica had been wearing her hair the same way for as long as Nikki could remember.

"How about me?" Nikki asked. "Do I look different?" She sat down on the bed, crossing her legs under her.

"Yeah, you do," Erica replied. She squinted, regarding Nikki closely. "You look older somehow. And you seem sort of different, too. I'm not sure how, though."

"It's skating," Nikki said. "It's really aged me." She was kidding, but in a way it was true. Being a member of Silver Blades had given her more confidence and poise than she'd had before. She certainly felt older than she had the last time she'd seen Erica.

"Ah." Erica nodded. "I see. So you'll be a shriveled-up old hag by the time you're seventeen?"

Nikki laughed. "Yep, that'll be me, all right."

Erica hunched over like an old woman, pretending to glide on skates while leaning on a cane. "It should be interesting, watching you tottering around on your skates." Both girls giggled.

Erica straightened up. She stared at the bulletin board that hung over Nikki's desk. It was covered with pictures of Nikki and her friends in Silver Blades. Most of the photos had been taken at competitions and ice shows.

"Wow," Erica said. "These are all your friends in Silver Blades, right? I feel like I know them already from your letters."

Nikki stood by her side. She pointed to a picture. "That's Tori holding up her medal when she took third place at the Regionals." She pointed to another pic-

ture and then another. "Here's Jill Wong at the Ice
Academy. And this one was taken when she and Amber had roles in *Nutcracker on Ice* last Christmas. And
this is Haley and her partner, Patrick."

"He looks just like Haley." Erica giggled. Patrick
had red hair and warm brown eyes—just like Haley.
They could almost be mistaken for brother and sister.

"It is funny, isn't it?" Nikki asked. In the photo,
Haley and Patrick were dressed up for their country-
and-western routine.

"And do you know who this is?" Nikki pointed to a
picture of a pretty Hispanic girl surrounded by Martina, Amber, Nikki, Tori, and Haley.

Erica studied it, then squealed with surprise. "Isn't
that Vanessa Guzman? The actress?"

"Yeah. Remember when I wrote to you that Martina
was the skating double for her movie? This was taken
during the filming."

"Wow. I can't believe you actually stood next to
someone famous. That's so incredible," Erica gushed.

"I guess." Nikki shrugged. "She wasn't one of the
nicest people I ever met, though."

"But still, she's rich, beautiful, and famous. I'll
never meet anyone like that." Erica gazed at the
photo, nearly breathless with admiration. "And Martina's almost famous, too, being in a movie and all."

"Well, you can meet *her* tomorrow at the rink."

Erica's eyes shone. "I can't wait. I want to ask her
what it's like to hang out with movie stars. Maybe she
can get me Vanessa Guzman's autograph."

"Maybe," Nikki said. "But I doubt it. Martina and Vanessa weren't exactly big friends."

"And what about Amber?" Erica asked. "Do you think I could get her autograph?"

"Amber's? Why would you want *her* autograph?" Nikki asked in surprise. "I mean, she's just a little kid."

"Yeah, but she had a huge part in *Nutcracker on Ice.*" Erica closed her eyes. "Imagine being on national TV when you're only eleven! I bet she'll be a big star someday."

"Hey, wait a minute. Alex and I are going to be big stars someday. Don't you want our autographs, too?" Nikki said, teasing.

Erica looked thoughtful. "Maybe you're right," she said. "And I should get Tori's as well. Didn't you tell me she's really good? I should have brought a little notebook or something. Then I could get everybody's and have them all together."

Nikki pictured Erica running around the rink asking for autographs. It was kind of sweet, the way she was so impressed with everything. But it was kind of embarrassing also—as if Erica was almost *too* impressed with everyone.

Erica studied the picture of Tori again. "Tori is really pretty," she said. "I wish I had blond hair like that. Didn't you tell me her new stepfather is some big shot?"

"Her future stepfather," Nikki corrected. "He's Roger Arnold, the owner of Arnold's, the chain of department stores. Her mom is a fashion designer. Roger has opened boutiques of her clothes in a lot of his stores."

"Wow," Erica breathed. "That's so romantic! Plus they must be really rich."

Nikki thought about Tori's big house and her huge wardrobe. "Yeah," she said. "You could say that."

"Wait until I tell Tori we shop at Arnold's back home," Erica said enthusiastically. "Maybe my mom even has some of her mom's clothes." She laughed. "I mean, the clothes her mom *designed*. You know what I mean. Except my mom could probably only buy them if they were marked down to half price or something."

"Um," Nikki said, "maybe you shouldn't tell Tori that."

"Why?" Erica asked.

"I don't know." Nikki said. "I just wouldn't, that's all." She couldn't say what she was really thinking— that Erica was gushing a little too much. Tori would definitely think Erica was uncool. And when Tori felt superior to someone—well, watch out, Nikki thought.

Nikki felt a little twinge of anxiety. She would never hurt Erica's feelings—not for the world. But what if her new friends thought her old friend was kind of a nerd?

Erica turned away from the bulletin board. "I just can't believe you hang out with these guys. But how come there aren't any pictures of you and Alex here? Where are they?"

"Oh, boy," Nikki said. "You asked for it." She picked up a photo album from her bookshelf. Sitting on the bed, she flipped to one of the pages near the back of the book. "Here we are at the Silver Blades ice show last year." She pointed to a photo of herself and Alex, both dressed in dark blue skating outfits. They stood at the center of the ice, smiling broadly, clasped hands raised over their heads.

"Ooh," Erica exclaimed. "Cool." She sat down next to Nikki, and Nikki felt a rush of affection for her.

Maybe Erica wasn't as sophisticated as her new friends, but it was nice to be admired. "You guys *do*

25

look like real stars," Erica said. She studied the picture more closely. "Hey, Alex looks even cuter in this picture than he does in the one you sent me."

"He's okay."

"He looks better than okay to me," Erica teased. "I know, though—you're going out with Kyle."

Nikki snorted. "I haven't written to you in a while, huh?"

"Not for, like, a month, you creep," Erica said. "What happened?"

"Nothing happened. Nothing ever happens. Kyle and I hardly ever see each other anymore." Nikki flipped the pages of the photo album, then closed it.

"So you broke up?"

"No, not officially. But he's always busy with hockey, and I'm always busy with skating. Things just kind of fizzled out."

"Do you still like him?"

"I guess," Nikki said. "I mean, I do like him, but we never really got that close. Kyle is a hard person to get to know. I kind of doubt we'll get back together."

Erica folded her hands behind her head and lay back on the bed. "I still think you should go out with Alex. You get to see *him* all the time, don't you?"

"Constantly. But you know why I don't want to go out with Alex. I mean, I like him, but not *that* way. Besides, if we were dating, I'd be afraid it would mess up our skating. It's better if we're just friends." Nikki paused. She was about to add that Alex was seeing Haley, anyway. But Erica interrupted.

"Well, at least you had a boyfriend for a while. I'll probably die of old age before I even go on a date."

"Aw, come on, Erica, it can't be that bad."

"Sure it can. I'm not like you. I'm just plain old me."

Nikki picked up a stuffed elephant from the bed. Erica *was* kind of plain, but this was the first time Nikki had ever heard her mention it. Or complain about it.

"Is there anyone you want to ask you out?" Nikki fully expected Erica to say no, nobody in particular. As far as Nikki knew, Erica had never even liked a guy.

Erica sat up. "Brandon. Brandon Quake. He is so awesome." She sighed deeply. "He's in ninth grade, he's got blond hair, and he looks kind of like Brad Pitt. Gorgeous eyes. Gorgeous mouth. Gorgeous everything. Every girl in school wants to go out with him."

"You actually have a crush on someone?" Nikki said in surprise.

"A megacrush." Erica sighed again.

"Well, is he going out with anyone?"

"No, not right now. At least not seriously."

"Wow," Nikki said. "So what's the problem? Go for it."

Erica made a face. "Oh, please. He'd never look twice at me. He'll probably end up with some cheerleader or something." She sighed again.

"Do you ever talk to him?" Nikki asked.

"Sure, all the time. We work together on the student council," Erica explained. "He's the president, and since I'm the secretary this year, I see him a lot. I'm always helping him get things done. And I think he likes me okay—to work with. But he'll never ask me out. Not in a million years." She took the elephant away from Nikki and smoothed one of its ears between her fingers.

"Does Brandon know you like him?" Nikki asked.

"Boy, I hope not!" Erica cried. "How embarrassing!"

"Well, you don't have to announce it," Nikki told her. "You could just flirt with him a little."

"Are you kidding?" Erica made a face. "Me flirt? Like I'd have a clue. . . ."

"Hmmm." Nikki frowned. It *was* hard to imagine Erica flirting. She was always so serious and quiet.

"You know what really stinks, though?" Erica asked, tossing the elephant back on Nikki's pillow. "I'm not sure how much longer we're even going to be working together. Brandon might get kicked off the council."

"Why?"

"Some of the teachers are really mad at him. A couple of weeks ago he wrote a column for the school paper saying this science teacher, Mr. Malloy, should be fired because he's really unfair to the girls. And he is, too." Erica's eyes blazed. "He only calls on boys in class, and he automatically gives them better grades. Everybody knows about it, but some of the teachers are acting like Brandon made the whole thing up. And they say that students shouldn't be allowed to criticize the teachers in the paper. S-me of them even say that Brandon's the one who should be fired—from the student council."

"Do you really think they'll do it?"

"I don't know." Erica shook her head. "At first they were just trying to get him to write an apology, but Brandon refused to do that. He thought it would be like saying the stuff he wrote about Malloy wasn't true. And it was. It's so unfair."

"Really," Nikki agreed. "Brandon sounds great, though—like he really sticks up for what he believes in. As my dad would say, he's got integrity."

"Totally," Erica agreed. "Integrity, character, all those heavy things." She moaned. "And he's so gorgeous, too!"

Nikki giggled. "You really *have* changed." She stood up. "I want to call Haley and Martina before it gets too late and tell them you're here."

Erica stood, too. "Okay. Maybe I'll go see if I can help your mom with Ben, if he's still awake." She left the room.

Nikki picked up the cordless phone that was lying in her room. She sat on the bed and called Martina.

"Hey, that's great," Martina said when Nikki told her about Erica. "I can't wait to meet her. But I can't stay on the phone. Richard needs to make some super-important call. He's standing here glaring at me." Richard was Martina's older brother.

"That's okay, Tee," Nikki said, using her special nickname for Martina. "I want to call Haley and Tori, anyway. I'll see you at the rink tomorrow."

Nikki hung up and dialed Tori. She quickly told her about Erica, and Tori agreed to help show Erica a fun time in Seneca Hills. Next Nikki called Haley.

"Haley, hi," Nikki greeted her. "Guess what? The greatest thing happened tonight." She rushed on before Haley could reply. "My friend Erica is here from Missouri. Remember, I told you about her. She's staying for a whole week!"

"Really? Neat," Haley replied. "Is she coming to the rink tomorrow?"

"Yeah." Nikki leaned back against her headboard. "I really want her to have a good time while she's here," she said. "I need to think of some fun things to do."

"Hmmm," Haley said. "You mean like the mall and the movies and the usual things?"

"Yeah. With the usual suspects—me, you, Tori, and Martina. But it would be fun to do something different, too."

"Sure," Haley said. "But don't you want to hear about Alex and our big date tonight? First we—"

Nikki didn't want to hear about it. "Wait!" she cried. "I just remembered—I promised to call Alex, and I forgot all about it! Sorry, Haley, but I've got to go!"

"But Nikki—" Haley started to protest.

"No, really, he made me promise to call," Nikki insisted. "I'll talk to you tomorrow, okay?"

"Okay," Haley said. "But if Alex says anything about me, you'd better call me right back. Especially if it's something good!"

"I will," Nikki promised. "Bye."

"Bye."

Nikki hung up. I *did* promise to call Alex, she told herself. But she also knew she couldn't bear to hear about the big date from Haley.

Nikki dialed Alex's number. He picked up right away.

"Hi. It's me," Nikki said quickly.

"Hi, me. It's about time you called. Did you forget?" Alex asked. He didn't sound mad.

"Sorry," Nikki said. "I did kind of forget. My parents had this surprise for me tonight—we went to the airport to pick up my friend Erica from Missouri. She's staying for a week."

"Cool," Alex said. "Anyway, it doesn't matter. If you had called, I would have been out. We didn't get home till almost nine o'clock."

"Oh." Nikki said. Nine o'clock was pretty late for Alex and Haley to be out when they had practice the next morning. "Anyway, I can't wait for you to meet Erica," Nikki went on. "Promise me you'll be really nice to her, okay? She's kind of shy and quiet. And—"

"Sure," Alex said. "No problem." Then he rushed on. "It was so funny at the mall tonight! They had

some actors pretending to be mannequins in one of
the store windows. Well, you should have seen Haley!
You know how crazy she is sometimes, so—"

"Yeah, I know," Nikki interrupted. Not Haley again!
She wanted to talk about Erica.

"Well, I didn't even notice the actors at first," Alex
continued. "I walked right by them. But not Haley!"

"Naturally," Nikki murmured.

Alex went on without a pause. "Haley knew what
was going on. So she got down on her knees in front of
the window, right by this guy who was sitting there
staring at the floor and acting like he wasn't real. And
she started making faces at him. He was trying so
hard not to laugh, but finally he just lost it. It was a
riot." Alex cracked up again.

Nikki laughed, too, in spite of herself. "That's Haley
for you."

"She is so much fun," Alex said. "Anyway, what I
wanted to ask you about earlier was, I was thinking
about bringing Haley a flower tomorrow. You know,
like a single rose or something. I bet she'd think it was
really cool. But I was wondering what her favorite—"

"I don't know, Alex," Nikki interrupted. "Why don't
you bring her one of those flowers that squirt water?
That's about her speed."

"Oh, gee, thanks, Nikki," Alex said sarcastically.
"You're a big help." He laughed.

"Sorry for teasing," Nikki said. "But Alex, about
Er—"

"Listen, Nik—I've got to go," Alex interrupted. "I didn't realize it was getting so late."

"Oh, okay. I'll see you at practice tomorrow," Nikki answered. Well, that was kind of rude, she thought as she hung up. He didn't let me say two words about Erica. All he could talk about was Haley, Haley, Haley.

Nikki stood up and stretched. Erica poked her head into the bedroom. "Your baby brother is too cute for words!" she exclaimed.

"Isn't he?" Nikki grinned. "You know, it's time for us to get to bed. We have to get an early start tomorrow." Nikki began to take the phone back to her parents' bedroom. "Oh!" she suddenly cried. "I forgot. I promised to call Haley back."

"But won't Haley be going to bed now, too?" Erica asked.

Nikki hesitated. She *had* promised. But it was getting pretty late.

"You're right," she finally told Erica. "It's silly to call. We'll see Haley at the rink in the morning."

"I'm so excited!" Erica gushed. "Tomorrow is going to be the best day ever."

"The best," Nikki echoed. She wasn't looking forward to seeing Alex and Haley together after their big date. She felt almost sick to her stomach at the idea. Why was she dreading it so much?

5

"This is even better than I expected," Erica said. She swallowed a yawn. "For five-thirty in the morning, that is." Erica sat next to Nikki on the bottom row of bleachers by the ice.

"Really?" Nikki pulled on a skate and tugged the laces. She yawned, her eyes tearing. She was tired. She and Erica had talked for a long time the previous night before they had finally fallen asleep. Nikki was paying for it now.

Nikki looked out at the ice. "There's Alex," she told Erica, pointing. Alex was already warming up. He glanced in Nikki's direction. His face broke into a huge smile, and he waved wildly.

"What a welcome," Erica said.

"Yeah," Nikki answered, feeling puzzled. She

started to wave back, but suddenly she heard Haley's voice beside her.

"Hi, Alex!" Haley called.

Nikki brought her hand down fast. How embarrassing! Alex was waving to Haley—not to her!

"Hi, Nikki." Nikki glanced up. Patrick, Haley's partner, stood in front of her.

"Hey, Patrick. This is my friend Erica," Nikki replied.

"Hi, Erica. Nice to meet you," Patrick said politely. "Want to warm up with me?" he asked Nikki. "They don't need us right now." He turned and pointed at the rink.

Nikki saw Haley skating over to Alex. Haley smacked her palm onto Alex's chest, then turned and sped away, laughing. Alex looked down at his chest. Nikki saw that Haley had planted a bright sticker on his sweater.

Alex burst out laughing. Then he chased after Haley. Finally he caught up with her, and they both slowed down and skated side by side.

"Do they practice together, too?" Erica asked.

"Uh, sure, sometimes," Nikki answered. "I mean, we're all friends." *Why don't I tell Erica the truth?* Nikki wondered. *Haley and Alex are a couple now.*

But somehow Nikki couldn't say the words. Instead, she lowered her head and pulled on her other skate. *It's not fair,* she thought suddenly. *It's just not fair that Haley can be so happy with Alex. She's got every-*

thing—skating talent, a great partner, and a boyfriend, too. Nikki couldn't help feeling a little jealous.

"Well, I'm off. See you later," Patrick said to Erica.

"I'd better get started, too," Nikki told Erica. "Are you sure you won't be bored watching?"

"Are you kidding? This is amazing," Erica insisted. She climbed into the bleachers to find the best seat.

Nikki finished tying her laces and quickly did her off-ice stretching routine. When she was finished, she removed her skate guards and stepped onto the ice. The other members of Silver Blades were beginning to arrive, and the ice was more crowded. She circled the rink slowly a few times.

Nikki moved into some easy jumps and spins. She knew she should go join Alex, but he and Haley were still fooling around. Nikki felt suddenly shy, as if she couldn't interrupt them. But she kept glancing in their direction.

They were having a great time. They even tried a couple of flying camel spins. They were totally out of sync.

They look terrible together, Nikki thought. Instantly she was ashamed that the thought made her happy.

Haley finished her spin and skated over to Alex. Playfully she reached out and pushed him away. As he glided backward he reached out and grabbed both of Haley's hands to stop himself. Haley crashed into him. She gazed up at Alex, and for a horrible moment Nikki thought he was going to bend down and kiss her right then and there.

"Hey, Alex!" Nikki blurted out. She sped across the ice. Alex looked up, startled.

"Hey, Nik," he said. He dropped Haley's hands.

"Hi, you guys," Nikki said to both of them. She turned to Alex. "Sorry I'm a little late. I, uh, had a cramp in my leg, and I was trying to work it out."

"That's okay," Alex smiled down at Haley. "Haley kept me company."

"Yeah," Haley teased. "He was so pitiful out here all by himself. There's nothing sadder than a pairs skater forced to skate alone." She punched Alex lightly in the arm.

"Oh, yeah, she felt really sorry for me," Alex teased back. "Look what she stuck on me." He pointed to the sticker on his chest.

" 'Cute but dumb,' " Nikki read. She made her own voice light and teasing. "Well, Alex, if the—"

"—shoe fits, wear it," Haley finished for her. "Or maybe I should say 'If the skate fits.' Anyway, I notice you haven't taken the sticker off. So it must be true."

Alex pretended to be insulted. "Well, I never turn down presents," he joked back. "No matter how tacky. Anyway, it's at least half true."

"Yeah—you *are* pretty dumb," Haley teased. She sped away, and Alex took off after her. He hooked an elbow around her neck. "Noogie time," he yelled, twisting his knuckles into Haley's head. She yelped and pulled at his arm until he let go.

"Come on, Alex," Nikki called. "Kathy's here."

"I'll get you back later," Haley promised Alex. She

skated away to join Patrick, who was warming up on the other side of the rink.

Nikki skated toward their coach. "We've got work to do," she called back to Alex over her shoulder.

"Yes, ma'am," Alex said, turning mock serious. He gave her a quick salute. "Let's get to work."

Kathy worked them hard for the next forty minutes, but they couldn't seem to do anything right.

Nikki frowned. I don't get it, she thought. We skated great yesterday. She pulled out of her double toe loop, trying to pretend she hadn't wobbled badly on her landing.

"Nikki Simon!" Kathy's voice cut across the ice, loud enough for every one of the Silver Blades members to hear. Nikki cringed.

"That is the sloppiest double toe loop I have ever seen you do." Kathy scowled. "You were way too far to the right on that landing. I'm surprised you could hang on to it at all."

Kathy was right. If she had fallen, it would have been the third time that day. Nikki's timing was terrible. She felt unfocused, completely off balance somehow. Even the death spiral had been all wrong. And that was a move she and Alex had supposedly mastered. Her body was supposed to be relaxed as he pulled her around, creating the fluid, graceful line that made a death spiral so beautiful to watch. Instead she'd felt as stiff as a board.

She glanced at Alex. They were skating side by side now, moving forward. They turned at the same time and skated backward. Nikki moved closer to Alex. He reached out, put his right hand around her waist, grabbed her right hand with his left, then lifted her above his head in a star-lift.

Alex got ready to release her right hand once she was up in the air. But that day Nikki held on. The lift felt shaky, and she wasn't going to risk crashing to the ice. Alex lowered her.

"Okay. That's enough," Kathy yelled across the ice. "Come over here."

They glided over to the coach. "What's going on with you two today?" Kathy asked. "You look terrible out there. Your edges are sloppy, and your timing is way off. I can't believe you're the same skaters I saw yesterday."

Nikki stared down at her skates. "I'm sorry," she mumbled. Most of their problems that morning had been her fault, not Alex's. And all three of them knew it.

"We just got off to a bad start," Alex offered. "It won't last."

"I certainly hope not," Kathy snapped. "Now get back out there and clean up your act."

"But practice is over," Nikki started to say.

"Take an extra five minutes," Kathy told her.

Nikki cringed. Focus, she told herself as she and Alex skated back to center ice. She took a deep breath. Focus, focus, focus.

Somehow they made it through the rest of their routine without any major disasters. Kathy dismissed them crisply. "I expect a vast improvement by this afternoon's session," she added.

"Me too," Nikki mumbled. She didn't watch as Alex skated off the ice. She slipped on her skate guards and turned toward the locker room. Suddenly Erica leaped up from her seat in the bleachers. "Nikki, wait up!" she called.

Nikki almost jumped. She'd forgotten all about Erica. Oh, no, she thought. Erica saw everything. And we skated so badly!

Erica swung herself down from the bleachers. "That was so awesome. You guys are great."

Nikki gave her a surprised look. She couldn't be serious! But Erica seemed totally sincere.

Erica lowered her voice. "Alex is so cute! Even cuter than his picture. You are so lucky."

"Yeah, right," Nikki said. She didn't feel lucky at all. "Come on, I'll introduce you to everyone." She led Erica into the locker room.

Tori, Martina, and Haley had already taken over their usual corner of the room. Nikki hoped they weren't talking about Haley and Alex's date.

"Hey, guys," Nikki called. "This is Erica, my best friend from Missouri." She pushed Erica forward. "This is Tori, Martina, Amber, and Haley," she said, pointing them out.

"Hi." Erica smiled shyly. "I saw you all skating out there. You're fantastic. I love your skating dress, Tori."

"Thanks," Tori said. "It's nothing special." As

usual, while everyone else wore leggings and sweat-shirts or warm-up suits, Tori had on a gorgeous outfit. Tori's mother believed that Tori should dress like a champion every day, not just when she was compet-ing.

The dress Tori was wearing that day was white, with a ruffled skirt, long sleeves, and a sweetheart neckline. It was covered with lace trim.

Tori checked Erica out. "Interesting sweatshirt," she said.

Nikki winced. She was suddenly painfully aware that Erica was wearing her teddy bear sweatshirt again. Why did she have to wear that silly thing? she wondered.

But Erica just smiled. "Thanks, Tori," she said.

"It's really great you could come visit," Martina quickly added. "We'll have to think of some fun stuff to do."

"Yeah," Haley said. "Something besides getting out of bed at the crack of dawn to watch us practice. I can't believe you came down here so early."

"Well, I couldn't wait to see Nikki skate," Erica con-fessed.

"She and Alex are pretty good, aren't they?" Amber asked.

"Hey, look, guys, I've got an idea," Tori cut in. "You want to come over to my house after practice tonight? We can order pizza and hang out. My mom's going out to dinner with Roger, and this will give me an excuse not to go with them. I got a new makeup kit at the mall yesterday. Maybe we can give each other make-overs."

"Sure," Nikki said. "That sounds like fun."

"Count me in," Martina said.

Amber shook her head. "Sorry, I can't make it. I have to meet my friend Tiffany. She's visiting me for the rest of this week. So I won't be able to come to your sleepover on Saturday night, Nikki."

"I can't make it, either," Haley put in. "Tonight I'm going to the movies with Alex. And Saturday night is just no good."

"What?" Nikki was surprised. "Why not?"

"Alex has to go to some party for his cousin. He said it's probably going to be a real bore, but his dad said he could bring one of his friends along. So he asked me."

"But you promised to come to my sleepover!" Nikki protested.

"Not really," Haley said. "I just said maybe."

"That's just great," Nikki said. "I don't believe this." She felt herself getting more and more upset.

"Look, I know I said I'd hang out with you guys. But give up a date with Alex just so I can put on makeup? Get real, Nikki." Haley tossed her head.

"She's got a point," Tori conceded.

"But . . ." Nikki stopped, not sure what she wanted to say. "I guess," she said finally. "If that's what you want to do."

Haley smiled broadly. "You bet," she said.

Nikki turned away and opened her locker. She pulled out her skate bag and clothes and quickly changed while Erica talked with the other girls. Nikki was angry, but she wasn't about to get into an argument with Haley. Especially not in front of Erica.

Soon the girls were all in the lobby, waiting for their rides home. Haley hurried toward Kathy's office to catch her ride. Erica turned to Nikki.

"Why didn't you tell me Haley's going out with Alex?" she asked.

"Because she isn't. I mean, not really." Nikki toyed with the zipper on her jacket.

"But I heard her say she has a date with him," Erica protested.

"Well, she's going to the movies with him. But it's no big deal," Nikki explained. "I told you, everyone in Silver Blades hangs out together. They're just friends."

"It sounded like more than that," Erica said.

"Well, it's not," Nikki insisted. "Haley was just joking around. She's always like that."

"Oh," Erica said. "Well, it's surprising. You'd think somebody would be going out with Alex. He's so cute." She frowned, thinking hard. "A guy like that shouldn't go to waste. He really shouldn't."

6

"**O**kay, girls, what's it going to be?" Tori asked. She picked up the phone, ready to dial. "Extra cheese, mushrooms, peppers . . ."

"Ugh, no mushrooms," Martina said. "And as far as I'm concerned, you can skip the peppers, too." She hoisted herself up onto a smooth marble countertop. They were in Tori's kitchen. The room was so sleek and modern, it could have been featured in a decorating magazine.

"Well, extra cheese, then?" Tori asked. "What do you think, Erica?"

"Oh, whatever you guys want is okay with me," Erica said. She had been really quiet ever since they'd arrived. Nikki had the feeling she was a little in awe of Tori's big, fancy house. She had stared wide-eyed at the two-story entrance hallway with its winding stair-case and huge chandelier. Tori's house sure wasn't like any of their friends' houses back in Missouri!

Nikki glanced at the digital clock on the gleaming white stove. It was a quarter after six. Alex and Haley were at the movies. She pictured them sitting together, Alex's hand reaching for Haley's in the dark. The numbers on the clock blurred before her eyes, and Nikki shook her head.

"Hey, earth to Nikki!" Martina snapped her fingers in Nikki's direction. "Didn't you hear Tori?"

"Uh, yeah, sure. Pepperoni is okay," Nikki said. "Whatever."

Martina rolled her eyes. "Okay, space cadet. Except we were discussing extra cheese."

"Oh, that's okay, too," Nikki said.

Martina smoothed back her long dark hair. "Extra cheese it is," she told Tori. "Just don't tell Sarge," she said to Erica. "It's not exactly the kind of low-fat, high-carbohydrate stuff she's always telling us to eat." She looked from Nikki to Tori. "So if I can't land my jumps tomorrow, I'm blaming you guys."

"Hey, no problem," Nikki answered. "You can just tell her it's all my fault. She's mad at me already, so what's the difference?"

"Bad practice, today, huh?" Martina said.

"Shhh, you guys, I can't hear," Tori complained.

They stopped talking while Tori ordered the pizza. Nikki opened a cupboard, pulled out a stack of plates, and put them on the table. Afternoon practice had been terrible, even worse than the morning. And this time it hadn't been all her fault, either. She'd caught Alex scanning the rink for Haley more than once. He hadn't been focusing any better than she had.

Nikki glanced at the clock. Six-thirty. In her mind, Alex slipped his arm around Haley's shoulder, pulling her close.

"I told them to deliver the pizza in an hour," Tori said, interrupting Nikki's thoughts. "That will give us some time to get beautiful. Let's go upstairs."

The girls bounded up the stairs. Nikki grinned at Erica's reaction as she entered Tori's room. Erica gaped at the deep rose carpeting, the plush draperies, and the antique brass-and-white-iron bed.

"Nikki, this room is amazing," Erica whispered.

"I know," Nikki whispered back.

Tori took a large blue box off her dresser. "Look at this," she said. "Twelve shades of eye shadow, six shades of eyeliner, four shades of blush, and eight shades of lipstick. Cool, huh?"

"Yeah," Nikki said, fingering an eye shadow brush. "Come on, Erica, sit down." She gestured to the chair by Tori's desk. "Let's do you first."

"Oh, no, that's okay," Erica said. "You guys go ahead. I never wear makeup."

"You mean you don't like it?" Tori asked. She set the makeup box down and plopped down on her bed.

"Um, no, that's not it. It's just . . . I don't think

there's much you can do with a face like mine." She shrugged.

"Wait a minute," Nikki said. "I object. I like your face."

"Well, thanks," Erica said. "But I'm not like you guys. I mean, you're all so pretty, and I'm just, well, plain old me."

Tori put a finger under Erica's chin and tipped her head up. She studied Erica's face. "I think you're selling yourself short," she said.

She turned to Nikki and Martina. "Remember the makeovers we had at the skating clinic this summer? I could do that for Erica."

Nikki was starting to get excited. "You mean a real, complete makeover?"

"Sure," Tori said. "Not just some new eye shadow, either. A whole new look."

"Do it," Nikki urged Erica. "This will really be fun." She tugged on Erica's ponytail. "First we should change your hair," she said.

"And do your nails, and maybe give you a facial," Martina added.

"Well," Erica said, "if you really want to . . ."

"We do," Nikki said.

"We could curl your hair," Martina suggested. "Do you have any hot rollers, Tori?"

"Sure. I'll get them."

"I know," Nikki said. "How about bangs? What do you think, Tee?"

"Wait!" Erica held up her hands in front of her forehead, as if Martina were ready to snip away. "What if they end up way too short or something?"

"Don't worry," Nikki reassured her. "Martina trims her little sister's bangs all the time. She's really good."

"It's true," Martina said. "My aunt taught me, and she's a hairstylist."

Erica pulled her hair out of its ponytail holder. She combed it down over her eyes with her fingers. "Well . . . ," she said, hesitating.

"Think about Brandon," Nikki told her.

"Who's Brandon?" Tori immediately asked. Martina leaned closer, too.

"He's this totally cool guy Erica likes back in Missouri," Nikki told them. "Only he hasn't asked her out or anything."

"Well, when I get through with you, the boys will be standing in line to ask for dates," Tori bragged.

Erica blushed. "All right," she finally said. "Go ahead. What have I got to lose?"

"Great!" Nikki exclaimed. "You're going to look fantastic."

Tori held up her makeover tools one by one, as if she were a surgeon about to operate. "Scissors, towel, comb, mirror," she recited. "And I have this vegetable mask—my mom uses it." She set everything down on the desk. "We should start with the facial, right?"

"Yeah," Nikki said. "And I can do your nails now, too." She took Erica's hand and began filing while Tori smeared the green stuff on Erica's face. As she worked, Nikki's mind wandered back to Haley and

Alex. The movie must be over by now, she thought. She pictured them walking out of the theater. Alex's head was bent to hear something Haley was saying. She imagined Alex laughing, then leaning down, his face close to Haley's. . . .

Suddenly Erica jerked her hand out of Nikki's grasp. "Hey," she said. "Aren't you supposed to leave a little nail on there?"

"Oops. Sorry." Nikki dropped the nail file. She picked up a bottle of polish and reached for Erica's hand again.

"You've been acting weird all night. What are you thinking about, anyway?" Tori asked Nikki.

"Nothing," Nikki told Tori. She felt her cheeks flame. She glanced away and caught Martina's eye. Martina gave her a puzzled look. Nikki dropped her eyes and pretended to be concentrating on coating Erica's nails with red polish.

Erica blew on her nails. "Boy," she said, "I'm really thirsty. Do you mind if I go get a drink of water?"

Nikki jumped up. "Stay right there," she said. "I'll get it." She dashed downstairs to the kitchen and filled a glass with water. She checked the clock. Twenty after seven. Maybe, she thought hopefully, Haley had a rotten time. Maybe she came home early.

She glanced at the phone. Well, why not? She set down the glass, picked up the phone, and dialed Haley's number. No answer. Not a good sign, Nikki thought. She hung up and turned around—and almost smacked right into Martina.

"Yikes!" Nikki cried.

"We decided we needed sodas," Martina said. She eyed Nikki closely. "Who were you calling?"

"Haley. I just wondered if she was home yet."

"But she and Alex went to the movies."

"Yeah, I know," Nikki said. "I wanted to see how their date was."

"And you had to find out right this minute?" Martina gave her a funny look. "I get the feeling you're not telling me the truth. But I can't figure out why."

"Well . . ." Nikki hesitated. Martina was her best friend in Silver Blades. They were almost as close as she and Erica used to be.

"Okay," Nikki blurted out. "I am upset. It's just that Alex forgot all about his plans with me the other day because he wanted to go out with Haley. And she wouldn't change the date to another night, and then she didn't come tonight because of Alex. And she canceled the plans we made for Saturday night so that she could go to some dumb family party with him." Nikki took a deep breath. "Suddenly all Alex talks about is Haley. And we've been messing up in practice like crazy. It's like now that they're together, I'm not important anymore."

Martina went to the refrigerator and pulled out four sodas. "Whoa," she said. "Slow down. You think you and Alex are having skating problems because he's dating Haley?"

"Well, yeah, maybe. Everything was fine before

that." Nikki picked up the water glass and ran her finger around the edge.

"Don't you think you're overreacting?" Martina asked. "Why are you so worried, anyway? Haley and Alex are just having fun."

"But you said Haley was in love," Nikki pointed out.

"I was *kidding*, dummy!" Martina gave Nikki a nudge. "Sure, Haley's excited—wouldn't you be if a cute guy like Alex started paying a lot of attention to you?"

"I guess."

"So relax. And don't worry so much about the skating. You guys are pros. Everybody has bad days."

"I know." Nikki smiled.

"Come on," Martina said. "I already finished Erica's bangs. Tori's putting on her makeup. Let's go see how she looks."

"Thanks, Tee," Nikki said. "I feel lots better."

"Wow!" Nikki exclaimed when they walked back into Tori's room. Tori was brushing out Erica's long curls. "You look fantastic!"

"Can I see?" Erica reached for a small mirror on Tori's desk.

"No, wait," Tori said. "I want to do something else first. That sweatshirt has got to go. It just doesn't fit your new image." She went to her closet and started pulling out clothes.

"But I thought you liked it," Erica said.

"I didn't say I liked it. I said it was *interesting*," Tori corrected. "It would be great if you were ten years old. But I think you need something a little more sophisticated."

Nikki tried not to giggle. It was exactly what she thought—but only Tori would say it so bluntly!

"Here, try this." Tori pulled out a turquoise shirt and a long skirt. "You're about my size, and I bet this color will look great on you."

Just then the doorbell rang. "That must be the pizza," Tori said. She handed Erica the clothes. "You change, and I'll go pay for it."

In a couple of minutes Erica was dressed. "Okay," Nikki said. "Now you can see yourself." She opened Tori's closet door all the way, revealing a full-length mirror.

Erica gasped. "Is that really me?" She reached up and touched her hair, which fell in soft waves to her shoulders. She turned first to her right, then to her left. Her face was glowing.

Tori hurried back into the room. She stopped short when she saw Erica. "That's *plain* Erica?" she teased.

"Not anymore," Nikki said. "It's amazing," she added, staring at Erica. "I've known you forever, but I never realized you have such pretty eyes. Wait until Brandon sees you now."

"He'll die!" Erica said. Then the smile left her face. "Oh, no! I'll never be able to do this by myself!"

"Sure you will," Tori assured her. "It's easy. We can

teach you how to put on makeup. And you can borrow those clothes for a while if you want."

"Oh, I couldn't do that," Erica protested.

"Why not?" Nikki asked. "Tori's got more clothes than she knows what to do with. She can live without them for a few days."

"Well, if you're sure it's okay . . ." Erica checked out her image in the mirror again, and a huge grin spread across her face. "I brought some baby-sitting money with me. Could you guys help me buy some new clothes before I leave?"

"Sure," Nikki said. "We could go to the mall tomorrow. Kathy called practice early, so we'll be done by three o'clock." She giggled. "I'd love to be there when Brandon sees you."

"Yeah," Erica said. "Wouldn't that be something?"

"Hold on," Martina said. "You should never talk about cute guys on an empty stomach. And I'm about to pass out here."

"Me too," Tori said. "Come on—you can tell us more over pizza."

"You guys go on down," Nikki said. "I'm just going to call my mom and tell her what time to come get us."

The other girls rushed downstairs, chatting and laughing. When they were gone, Nikki dialed Haley's number.

Just to see how things went, she told herself. Not that it's any big deal. Martina's right—Haley just has a little crush. Alex will get interested in some other girl, and Haley will forget all about him.

Haley answered on the first ring. "Hi, Haley," Nikki said, trying to sound casual. "How was the movie?"

"Incredible!" Haley said. "Alex is so sweet. He brought me a daisy. And he held my hand the whole time."

"Oh." Nikki felt her stomach drop.

"You know what's so great about Alex?" Haley asked.

"No, what?" Nikki managed to say.

"I can talk to him about anything. He's really fun, but I can be serious with him, too. He really listens to me. We went to Super Sundaes after the movie, and before I knew it, I was telling him how I felt about my parents' separation. I never talked to a guy like that before." Haley was silent for a moment.

"You can always talk about that stuff to me, you know," Nikki said.

Haley didn't seem to hear her. "Alex is so incredibly nice," she said. "And romantic! Why didn't you tell me how great he was? I think he might just be perfect."

"I'm not sure I'd go that far," Nikki replied.

"No? Listen to this," Haley said. "When we got home, he came inside with me for a minute. We were standing there, talking about practice tomorrow, and then he took both my hands in his and kind of held them for a minute. And then . . ." Haley paused.

"What?" Nikki held her breath. She wasn't sure she wanted to hear the answer.

"He kissed me! My first real kiss. It was fantastic. It was—"

Nikki interrupted her. "That's great, Haley. I'm really happy for you. But I've got to go now. I'll call you tomorrow, okay?"

She hung up before Haley could say another word. There was a sick feeling in her stomach. And somehow she knew it was only going to get worse.

7

Nikki boosted herself up just as Alex lifted her, his hands around her waist. He threw her, and Nikki pulled in and tried to complete the two and a half revolutions of the double axel. She made the rotations, but she hit the ice too hard and fell in an awkward heap.

"Hold it! Stop right there!" Kathy skated across the ice to Nikki and Alex. It was Wednesday morning. Nikki had been trying to skate her best, but the moves just weren't coming.

At least Erica wasn't there to watch. Nikki would have been mortified if her friend had seen her skate this badly.

Nikki stood up, rubbing her bruised hip. It was the fourth time she and Alex had blown the double axel. The first time, Nikki hadn't jumped high enough to

tention to our routine and less attention to her, we might get somewhere."

Alex clenched and unclenched his fists. "Leave Haley out of this," he said. "She's got nothing to do with it."

"Right," Nikki countered. "And Sarge didn't mean *you* when she was giving that little lecture about concentration and dedication. It was all for my benefit, I suppose." She started to skate away, but Alex grabbed her arm, stopping her.

"Maybe not," he said. "But you know what? Your attitude really stinks."

Nikki shook her arm out of his grip. "What's wrong with my attitude?"

"You used to be fun to skate with. But lately you come out here every day acting like you're mad at the world, like you're facing some kind of torture test. It's not fun anymore, Nikki, and it shows in our skating. No way that's my fault." Alex turned and skated off.

Nikki was stunned. She stood for a moment, watching Alex's back, then turned and skated hard to the edge of the rink. Hot, angry tears stung her eyes. How could Alex be so mean? It wasn't her fault they were having so much trouble. He was the one who seemed more interested in his love life than in skating, not her.

Nikki blinked hard several times to stop the tears. She stepped off the ice, put on her skate guards, and walked slowly into the locker room.

Martina, Haley, and Tori were there, changing into

their street clothes. Amber had left early with her friend Tiffany. Nikki didn't want to talk to any of them. She sat down on the bench and undid her skate laces, her head down.

"Hey, Nikki," Tori said. "You ready to hit the mall this afternoon?"

Nikki forced herself to look up and smile. "Sure," she said. "It'll be fun. Erica's psyched."

"Great." Tori nudged Haley. "How about you? Are you coming?"

Haley pulled a ponytail holder out of her red hair. "Coming where?"

"We're going to the mall," Nikki said. "Erica wants us to help her pick out some new clothes."

"Yeah," Martina said. "We did this awesome make-over on her last night. Wait until you see her!"

"Cool," Haley said. "But I can't go today. I've got some stuff I have to do."

Nikki couldn't believe it. Not again! "What kind of stuff?" she asked.

"I'm going to Alex's house tonight," Haley explained. "We're renting a movie. I want extra time to get ready."

Tori folded the green skating dress she'd worn for practice and put it in her bag. "To get ready? What are you going to do—polish your combat boots?"

Haley made a face at her. "Very funny," she said. "For your information, I'm going to wash my hair and figure out what to wear. I don't want to be rushed, that's all."

"That won't take all afternoon," Nikki said. "You could come for a while, at least."

"Sorry, I really can't." Haley pulled on her sweatshirt.

"But this is important. You've hardly even met Erica," Nikki protested.

"Alex is important, too," Haley said. "To me."

"So you think you should completely ignore your friends because of Alex?" Nikki asked.

Haley turned away, not even answering her. Suddenly the locker room fell silent.

"Well," Tori said finally, picking up her bag and slinging it over her shoulder, "you can always change your mind. Call me if you need a ride—my mom's going to drive. I'll see you guys this afternoon."

Tori left. Haley sat down next to Nikki. "Look, I'm sorry about this afternoon," she said. "I *will* spend some time with you guys, I promise. Just not today."

"Uh-huh," Nikki muttered angrily.

Haley turned to Nikki and lowered her voice. "Did Alex say anything?"

"About what?" Nikki looked up.

Haley scraped at the bench with her fingernail. "You know," she said. "About our date last night."

"Oh," Nikki answered. "No."

"Hasn't he said *anything* to you about me—like about how much he likes me?" Haley sounded anxious.

Nikki pulled a comb out of her bag and ran it through her hair. "Uh-uh." She paused. A hard knot was forming inside her stomach. "He hasn't said any-thing," she said.

"Oh." Haley looked at Martina, then lowered her voice even more. "Did he tell you he kissed me last night?"

"No," Nikki answered. "I told you, he hasn't said anything. He hasn't even mentioned you." She threw the comb into her bag.

"But—" Haley began. Two small red spots appeared on her cheeks.

"Nikki . . . ," Martina said, a warning in her voice.

Nikki barely heard Martina. "But what? So Alex kissed you. Big deal. I bet it didn't mean *anything* to him. Alex probably kisses girls all the time. You know he's a giant flirt. Or did you forget?"

Haley stood up and took two steps away from Nikki. Her cheeks were flaming, and her brown eyes flashed. "He is not!" Her voice was quiet but fierce. "Not any-more." She took another step backward and almost tripped over her skate bag. She picked it up and slammed it down on the bench. "What's your prob-lem, anyway?" she asked, not bothering to keep her voice low now. "Can't handle somebody going out with your partner? Why don't you just grow up?"

"Hey, guys," Martina interjected. "Calm down." She touched Haley's arm, but Haley shook her off.

"Don't tell me to calm down. Did you hear her?" she asked Martina. "What *is* her problem, anyway? Do you know?"

Martina looked from Haley to Nikki and back again. "I, um . . ."

"I'll tell you what my problem is," Nikki countered. "I'm sick of watching you make a fool of yourself over Alex. Everybody knows what he's like, Haley. But you act like the two of you are Romeo and Juliet." She shoved her arms into her jacket and shrugged it up over her shoulders. " 'Alex kissed me,' " she mimicked, her voice high and sickly sweet. She fluffed her hair with her hand and made a face. " 'I have to stay home and fix my hair for Alex.' " She glared at Haley. "I'm sick of it," she said again. "I wish you two weren't even going out."

Haley looked as stunned as if she'd been struck. Nikki picked up her bag, whirled around, and stormed out of the locker room.

8

"**H**ey, Nikki, listen to this," Erica said. She was lying on Nikki's bed with her feet propped up on the wall. A *Seventeen* magazine was in her hands. Nikki had been home from morning practice for an hour or so. She and Erica had only a little time to kill before Nikki had to be back at the rink for her second practice.

"What?" Nikki asked.

"There's an article in here called 'Seven Ways to Grab His Attention.' Maybe I could use this on Brandon." She flipped through the magazine, searching for the right page.

"Maybe," Nikki said. She sat on the floor, carefully painting her nails with pale pink polish. If only *her* biggest problem were getting some boy to notice her! She was beginning to have some regrets about blowing up at Haley. She'd been hoping to ask Tori, Martina, and Haley over for a sleepover on Friday night instead of Saturday night. But the way things were now, Haley would probably refuse to come. Nikki would have to swallow her pride and apologize.

Somehow she was going to have to cool her anger at Alex, too, before practice. She had to show him he was wrong—she wasn't always in a bad mood. She'd be a little ray of sunshine on the ice that afternoon, even if it killed her.

Erica interrupted her thoughts. "Here it is," she said. She read silently for a minute. "Boy, is this lame. Listen to this. 'One: Accessorize.' Oh, please. They want me to carry a Game Boy or a Pez dispenser or something, to start a conversation. No way. Brandon would think I'd lost my mind." She took her feet off the wall and rolled over. " 'Two: Pop a question.' Forget that, too. I've asked Brandon plenty of questions. All he does is answer them—and then ignore me." A wistful look flitted across Erica's face. "According to the article, he's supposed to answer me, then gaze longingly into my eyes, fall down on his knees, and ask me out."

Nikki forced a smile. "Right," she said.

"Ha! I wish!" Erica scanned the article. "How about this? 'Number five: Time in. Lightly touch his wrist with one finger when you ask him the time.' Hmmm. Maybe I could do that. I wonder if he'd notice. Or this one: 'Six: Give him a nickname.' His friends already call him Earthquake, you know, because his last name is Quake. Let's see . . . Brandon . . . Branman?"

Erica giggled. "Sounds like a cereal. Maybe Branster?"

"That rhymes with *hamster*," Nikki murmured.

"Okay, forget that," Erica said. "How about number seven: 'Ask him a favor.' "

Nikki blew on her nails to dry the polish. "Yeah, like, 'Brandon, could you do me a big favor and take me to the prom?' " she suggested. " 'Or marry me?' "

Erica started giggling. Nikki cracked a smile.

"Oh, well," Erica said, and closed the magazine. "These things never really help."

The phone rang. "I'll get it," Nikki said. She grabbed the phone and talked for a second. "It's your mom," she said, handing the phone to Erica.

"Wow," Erica said when she hung up. "You won't believe this!"

"What?" Nikki settled down on the floor.

"My mom said a boy called me. He didn't leave his name, though." Erica got up off the bed and paced around the room. "I wonder if it was Brandon."

"Has Brandon ever called you before?"

"Are you kidding? I don't get calls from guys, period. I don't know who else it could be, though. Unless it was Jason, the guy who sits next to me in chemistry. Sometimes he borrows my notes. But I don't see why he'd call me during vacation."

"Maybe you've got a secret admirer."

"Yeah, right," Erica said with a laugh. "If it was Brandon, he probably had some grunt work that needed to be done for the student council. Still, I wish I'd been there . . . I told my mom to find out who it was if he called again."

Nikki stood up. "Well, maybe it *was* Brandon," she said. "Maybe he finally realized that the girl of his dreams is right under his nose."

Nikki held up a fuzzy pink sweater. "What do you think?" she asked Martina. They were at Canady's, their favorite clothing store in the mall.

"Too cutesy-pie," Tori said firmly. "I'll find something better." She took the sweater from Nikki's hands, put it back, and went to search another rack of clothing nearby.

Tori, Nikki, and Martina were waiting outside the dressing room while Erica tried on clothes they'd picked out. When Tori left, Martina turned to Nikki. "Is anything wrong?" she asked. "You seem kind of upset."

"Yeah, well, I guess I am," Nikki admitted.

"You want to talk about it?" Martina asked.

"Oh, Tee, it's just everything," Nikki said. She was surprised when tears welled up in her eyes. "Alex and I are going to really blow it at the Ice Theater. We can't do anything right together. Did you see us at practice today?" she asked, then rushed on. "I thought

Kathy would explode into a million pieces. We were so awful!" She groaned. "If only Alex weren't going out with Haley."

"Huh?" Martina said. "I can't believe you're still thinking about that! What difference does it make?"

"It makes all the difference," Nikki insisted. "Don't you see? Alex is too girl-crazy to pay attention to our skating. I get mad, and then we can't get anything right." She sniffled.

Martina sighed. "I don't get it. How come you're so jealous?"

"Jealous!" Nikki exploded. "I'm not jealous. I just care about my skating."

"It doesn't sound that way," Martina said carefully. "But maybe you just need to calm down a little." She paused. "I hate to say this, but whatever is going on between Haley and Alex is really between them."

"I don't believe it. You think I'm being selfish," Nikki said.

"Well," Martina said, "a little. I could understand if you were worried about Haley—I mean, if you thought that Alex was going to hurt her or something. But you're only thinking about yourself."

"And about our skating performance," Nikki protested.

"I think you just need to relax, okay?" Martina said in a more cheerful voice. "This ice show is a big deal. You have every right to care about it. But don't confuse that with your friendships."

"Maybe you're right," Nikki said. "Okay. I'll try."

Nikki felt suddenly ashamed of herself. Martina *was* right. She had been kind of selfish. From now on, she'd try to be happy for Haley and Alex.

Just then Erica appeared, wearing a pale green slip dress over a white baby T-shirt. "What do you think?" she asked.

"Perfect," Tori said. "It really shows off your legs." Martina nodded in agreement.

"I wasn't sure you *had* legs," Nikki teased. "I haven't seen you in a dress since we graduated from elementary school."

"I know," Erica said. "My mother will faint when she sees this." She twirled in front of the mirror. Her hair swung out and then rested in soft curls on her shoulders. "I can't believe how different I look," she said. "I really owe you guys."

"Forget it," Tori said, but she was obviously pleased.

"I wish you could all come home with me," Erica told them. "I'm going to make my mom take me on a major shopping spree. But I'm still not sure that I can do it on my own."

"Sure you can," Tori said encouragingly. "Just hold things up and say to yourself, 'Would Tori Carsen wear this?' If it doesn't pass the Tori test, put it back."

Erica laughed. "I guess I'll have to burn everything in my closet. I don't think anything I have will pass."

"Just promise me one thing," Tori said. "No more teddy bear sweatshirts."

"Got it," Erica said.

"Anyway," Nikki said, "with the skirt and sweater we picked out before, you have two perfect outfits."

"Yeah, and I can't afford anything else," Erica said.

"So change your clothes and let's hit Super Sundaes. I'm starving!" Nikki finished.

"The bottomless pit speaks!" Martina teased.

Fifteen minutes later they were all seated in a booth at Super Sundaes, waiting for their orders.

"My mom said the sleepover Friday night is okay with her," Nikki said. "Can you guys come?"

"You bet," Tori answered. "I'm ready to party."

"How about you, Tee?" Nikki asked.

"Definitely. Is Haley coming?"

"I don't know," Nikki said. She and Haley had avoided each other at afternoon practice. Nikki knew she still had to apologize, but she hadn't been able to make herself do it yet.

"You want me to call her?" Martina offered. "You know, play peacemaker?"

Nikki brightened. "Would you? Do you think it would work?"

"Hey, what are you guys talking about?" Tori asked.

"Yeah, did you and Haley have a fight or something?" Erica asked.

Nikki picked up a spoon and toyed with it. "Yeah. I kind of blew up at her over nothing." She sighed. "I was having a bad day, and I guess I took it out on Haley."

Suddenly the girls heard familiar voices. "Hey, Patrick, look who's here. Four gorgeous babes just dying for a little company." It was Alex. Patrick McGuire was with him.

Tori, Martina, and Nikki all groaned. "You know," Tori said, "we were having a perfectly good time—"

"Without us?" Alex interrupted. "Never!"

"You wish," Nikki retorted. She slid over to let Alex sit down. Tori and Erica made room for Patrick.

Patrick leaned around Tori to speak to Erica. "Hi, Erica," he said. "I almost didn't recognize you. You look great."

"Wait a sec, McGuire," Alex jumped in. "You know this beautiful creature? Why don't you introduce me?"

"Beekman, you nerd," Patrick retorted. "This is Erica, Nikki's friend from Missouri, remember? Nikki introduced us to her at the rink yesterday."

"No way," Alex said. "I never forget a pretty face. It's a special talent of mine." Alex grinned at Erica.

Nikki exchanged a glance with Martina. *And Haley thinks he isn't a flirt?* Nikki's look said.

For a minute Nikki wished Haley were with them. If she saw the way Alex was acting, she'd know that a date with Alex didn't mean as much as she thought.

Erica blushed and giggled. "We did meet," she said. "I saw you skate."

"Ah," Alex said. "Another special talent of mine. I hope you were really impressed."

Erica giggled again. "Oh, I was impressed. You're terrific."

Alex beamed. "Not only is she beautiful, but the lady recognizes great skating. Of course, I *am* wonderful. . . ."

"Like when?" Nikki asked in a teasing voice.

"Hey, I'm good, too," Patrick said to Erica. "Did you see me?"

"Uh-huh," Erica said. "I saw you and Haley doing a . . . what do you call it? A death spiral? It was cool."

"Thanks," Patrick said proudly. "We're really good at that."

"Hey, so are we," Alex protested. "Nikki and I do a fantastic death spiral."

Not lately, Nikki thought. But it was nice that Alex was bragging about *her* for a change instead of talking about Haley.

"You know," Tori observed, "it's amazing either of you can skate at all."

"What do you mean?" Patrick asked.

"You'd think those big swelled heads of yours would throw you off balance," she joked.

"Yeah!" Martina swayed in her seat and dropped her head down on the table with a clunk to demonstrate. "Like that." The girls burst out laughing.

They were still laughing when the waitress arrived with their frozen-yogurt sundaes. Patrick reached over to the empty booth behind them and snatched a spoon from a place setting.

"Oh, no, you don't," Nikki said. "This is all mine."

She moved her sundae closer to her and wrapped her arm around it. Martina and Tori did the same.

"Ah, come on," Patrick pleaded, his spoon poised in midair. "Share with your buddy."

"Here, Patrick," Erica said. "You can have some of mine." She pushed her sundae a little closer to him.

Nikki was puzzled. Was Erica flirting with Patrick? Couldn't be, she told herself. Erica's not the type.

Patrick grinned. "All right," he said. "Now there's a real friend. And she's cute, too."

"Hey, how about me?" Alex looked hurt.

"You're not so cute," Tori teased.

Alex made a face at her. "Very funny. I meant the frozen yogurt. Who's going to share with *me*?"

Erica scooped a huge mound of frozen yogurt, whipped cream, and chocolate sauce onto her spoon. "Open wide," she said, and shoveled it into Alex's mouth. He opened his eyes comically wide and pretended to have trouble swallowing it all. A small blob of whipped cream dripped down his chin.

Erica reached across the table and dabbed at Alex's chin with her napkin. She rolled her eyes at Nikki. "Remind you of anything?" she asked. "Like feeding Ben, maybe?"

"Yeah," Nikki said. She was amazed at Erica. This was the girl who didn't have a clue about flirting? That magazine article must have helped more than she thought.

Erica grinned at Alex. "He needs a little yogurt on

his clothes and in his hair. Then he'll really look like Ben!"

"That could be arranged," Patrick said. He pulled back the tip of his spoon with one finger and aimed at Alex.

Tori grabbed it away from him. "You wouldn't dare!"

"You're right," Alex said, taking the spoon from Tori. "I wouldn't want Erica to think we're a bunch of immature slobs."

"Too late," Nikki wisecracked. "She knows that already."

"Speaking of the time . . ." Erica reached across the table and gently tapped Alex on the wrist. "Exactly what time is it, anyway?" she asked.

Nikki almost choked on her yogurt. Erica was practicing the hints from "Seven Ways to Grab His Attention"—on Alex!

And from what Nikki could see, Erica had done it. She had Alex's attention. And Patrick's, too! She gaped at Erica in astonishment. She couldn't believe it. The shy, plain friend who had stepped off the plane just a few days before had vanished. The new Erica was a boy magnet!

9

"**M**om! I'm home!" Nikki dropped her skate bag in the back hall. She hung up her jacket and hurried into the kitchen. The rich smell of her mom's chili filled the air.

It was Friday, the night of the sleepover. Practice hadn't gone well, but Nikki wasn't going to worry about that now. For once she was just going to have fun.

"Hi, Nikki," her mother said. "Are you ready for the big night?" She sliced a carrot into neat rounds.

"Yeah," Nikki said. "I can't wait for everyone to get here." Even Haley was coming. Martina had called her and smoothed things over. Then Nikki had finally apologized at practice that morning. Haley had promised to make it to the sleepover.

"Is that for us?" Nikki asked, pointing to the pot of chili.

"Yes," her mother answered. "And I'm making a salad. I still need to run to the mall, though, and get a couple more things. And the family room needs to be straightened up. And we need to move some furniture, too, if you're planning to sleep in there."

Nikki hurried over to the counter, picked up a slice of carrot, and popped it into her mouth. "Okay," she said. "I can do that. Where's Erica?"

"She's watching Ben for me. I think they're in the family room." Mrs. Simon dropped a handful of carrots into the salad. "You got some mail today—it looks like a videotape." She gestured toward a small table in the corner.

"Yes!" Nikki said. "This is the tape of last year's World Championships! Gilbert and Morris skate that great long program to 'The Impossible Dream' on it. I can't wait to watch it."

Erica strolled into the kitchen, carrying Ben. She was wearing one of the new outfits she'd gotten at Canady's: a long black skirt that clung to her narrow waist and then flared out at the bottom, and a cropped cherry red sweater. She looked totally amazing. Nikki still wasn't used to her new look.

"Watch what?" Erica asked.

"This." Nikki held up the tape.

"Let me guess . . . it's skating, right?"

"Of course," Nikki said. "What else?"

Erica stood Ben on the floor, letting him hold her

fingers, and walked him across the kitchen. After several steps he let go and plopped down on his diapered bottom. "Yay, Benny!" Erica cried, clapping her hands. He clapped, too, giggling with delight.

"You'll be walking in no time," Erica told the baby.

Mrs. Simon groaned. "Don't rush it," she said. "I have enough trouble keeping up with him already." She stirred the chili and put the lid on the pot. "Nikki, I'm afraid you'll have to put off watching that tape until later. I'll need your help with Ben at the mall. He's learned to wriggle out of the safety belt in his stroller, and he stands up every time I stop. I need you girls to keep an eye on him. Otherwise, I'm afraid he's going to crack his little head open."

"But Mom," Nikki protested, "you said the family room needs to be fixed up. And I've been waiting forever to watch this tape. Besides, somebody should be here in case anyone gets here early."

"I can watch Ben," Erica offered. "Nikki can stay here. I don't mind."

"Well . . ." Mrs. Simon hesitated. She looked from Nikki to Erica and then back again. "If you're sure."

"Are you kidding?" Erica said. "I love this kid." She kissed Ben on the top of the head. "Just try to tear me away from him."

"All right," Mrs. Simon said.

"Thanks, Erica!" Nikki said.

Erica and Mrs. Simon put on their coats and dressed Ben to go out. Nikki grabbed a handful of graham crackers out of the cupboard. She carried them with her tape into the family room. If she fixed up the family room quickly, she'd still have time to watch her tape.

Nikki picked up Ben's toys from the floor, tossed them into a basket, and moved it into the living room. Then she dragged the coffee table into the living room, too, to make some floor space for the sleeping bags. There, that should do it, she thought. She set up the VCR and settled down on the couch with the remote control and her crackers.

Fast-forwarding through the tape, she found Karen Gilbert and Michael Morris's performance. As the crowd applauded wildly, Gilbert and Morris skated to center ice, holding hands and smiling broadly. Their music began, and the pair moved into a slow face-to-face spin, then gracefully separated. Every move they made was perfectly timed and looked effortless. And the lifts! Michael Morris could hoist Karen Gilbert into the air as if she were a paper doll. She touched down flawlessly every time, too, and landed every jump he threw her into. But even more impressive, they managed to convey a level of emotion no one else could match.

At the end of the performance Nikki stopped the tape and sat without moving for several minutes. Suddenly she felt terrible. She rewound the tape to the throw double axel and watched again. The difference between Gilbert and Morris and herself and Alex was painful. Next to them, she and Alex skated like total geeks.

Frustrated, Nikki punched the stop button on the remote and then flung it down. She slumped forward on the couch. They had only eight days left to practice, and she and Alex were skating worse than ever. They couldn't skate this way in the Ice Theater show. They'd make fools of themselves. They'd embarrass Kathy, their friends, and every member of Silver Blades.

"It's going to be a total disaster," Nikki murmured.

She reached for the remote control and turned the tape back on. She watched the other routines, then rewound the tape to the beginning of Gilbert and Morris's program. When she reached their throw double axel, she ran it in slow motion several times. There was something. . . .

"That's it!" Nikki jumped up, excited. Gilbert and Morris had a completely different approach to the move. Especially Karen Gilbert. Nikki watched it again. Yes! Karen didn't hesitate as she lifted into her double axel. Nikki was always concentrating on preparing for the rotation—she was hesitating at the very moment when she should be launching herself fearlessly into the air!

She couldn't wait to tell Alex and practice it a new way. Nikki reached for the phone. Just then she heard a car in the driveway. Her mother and Erica were home. She leaped up and ran into the kitchen to greet them.

Her mother came in with Ben slung over one shoulder. He was sound asleep. "Would you take him?" she whispered to Nikki. "See if you can get a clean diaper on him and then get him into his crib." She lifted him gently over to Nikki's shoulder. "That will give me time to unload the car and finish the food for tonight. I thought I'd make some corn bread to go with the chili."

Nikki carried Ben upstairs to his room, careful not to jar him in any way. With one hand under his head, she laid him softly on the changing table. His eyelids fluttered, but he didn't wake up. It was amazing the way he could sleep through just about anything, she thought. She changed his diaper and carried him to his crib.

She hurried downstairs. Her mother was bringing in the last of the packages from the car. Nikki spotted a bakery box on the counter.

"It's a chocolate cake," her mother said.

"Yum! Thanks, Mom." Nikki glanced at the clock. "Yikes! I didn't know it was so late! Everybody will be here soon. I'd better get ready." She looked around, puzzled. "Where's Erica?" she asked.

"She's still at the mall," her mother answered. She stirred the chili and adjusted the heat. "She ran into Alex outside the movie theater. I guess he invited her to join him, because she asked me if she could stay for the movie. She was such a big help to me while we were shopping, I told her to go ahead. She deserved a little break. Alex and his dad will drop her off as soon as the movie's over. So she'll only miss a little of the sleepover."

Nikki stared at her mother in shock. "Erica is at the movies—with Alex?"

"Yes." Mrs. Simon took out a bowl and a few boxes from the cupboard.

Nikki swallowed hard. She couldn't believe Alex had asked Erica to the movies when he was supposed to be dating Haley. Haley would be so upset. And furious! How would she explain this to Haley? She checked the time again, feeling a wave of panic. She needed an excuse, some other reason to explain why Erica wasn't around. Maybe she could say she was upstairs, sick. Too sick even to come downstairs.

No, that won't work, Nikki realized. Haley might want to go see her. Maybe I could—

The doorbell rang.

Mrs. Simon glanced out the window. "Haley's here, with Martina and Tori," she announced.

Nikki stared helplessly at her mother.

"Nikki!" her mother called. "What's wrong with you? Don't just stand there. Go answer the door."

10

Nikki fought the urge to run upstairs and hide under the bed. While she was standing there trying to decide what to do, the doorbell rang again. Her mother stared at her. Nikki sighed and squared her shoulders.

She walked to the front hall and opened the door.

"Boy, what took you so long?" Tori complained. Tori and Martina burst into the hallway. Haley rushed in after them. Nikki met Haley's eyes for the briefest moment. Then she looked away. Haley was going to be really angry, she just knew it.

Tori, Martina, and Haley dropped their sleeping bags and backpacks and took off their jackets.

"It smells good in here," Martina said. "I bet Nikki was too busy stuffing her face to answer the door. Right, Nikki?"

Nikki smiled weakly.

"Where should we put this stuff?" Tori asked, lifting her jacket and sleeping bag.

"In the family room, I guess," Nikki said with a shrug, feeling totally uncomfortable. She had been feeling great that she and Haley were friends again. Now she couldn't even look at Haley.

"Hello! What's up?" Haley waved her hands in front of Nikki's face. "You have this weird dazed look."

"Nothing," Nikki said, squirming.

"Then smile! This is a party." Haley pushed up the corners of Nikki's mouth with her index fingers. "Like this," she teased. "Come on, you can do it."

Nikki grinned a little in spite of herself. She couldn't resist Haley's high spirits. "Okay," she said.

They entered the family room. "Hey, where's Erica?" Tori asked, looking around. Nikki's grin disappeared.

"Uh, she's . . . uh . . . ," Nikki stalled, trying frantically to think of a story that would hold water. "She went—she stayed—"

Her friends stared at her.

Nikki sighed. "She's at the movies," she blurted out. "With Alex." Nikki felt her cheeks burning. "She's at the movies with Alex. There. I said it."

Haley stared at her in shock. "*My* Alex?" she asked, her voice rising.

"He's not *your* Alex," Nikki answered automatically. Martina shot her a warning look. "At least, he isn't anymore."

"Let me get this straight," Haley said slowly. "Alex—the same Alex that I've been going out with—is on a date with your friend Erica. And even though you know how much I like him, you let her go?"

"I couldn't stop her," Nikki said. "I wasn't even there!"

Haley shook her head. For a minute she didn't say anything. Tori and Martina looked from Nikki to Haley without a word.

"I knew it," Haley finally said. "I knew you'd do something like this."

"I didn't do it," Nikki insisted.

"You've been jealous ever since I started seeing Alex," Haley burst out. "And I heard how she was falling all over him at the mall the other day. I bet you put her up to this."

"I did not!" Nikki said hotly. "I would never do that, and you know it!"

"Oh, yeah?" Haley glared at her. Nikki had never seen her so angry. "You said you wished Alex and I weren't going out. You and your stupid jealousy," she went on. "I wish you'd just grow up."

"Me?" Nikki said. She was almost yelling now. "You're the one who's acting like some second-grader. It's not my fault Alex is a flirt. It's not my fault he has to impress every girl who comes along. If he wants to go out with Erica, that's not my fault, either." She crossed her arms and glared back at Haley.

"I can't believe I ever thought you were my friend," Haley retorted. "But you're not. Not anymore."

"Wait a minute, Haley," Martina said. "I don't think Nikki would really—"

"Forget it!" Haley practically spat the words out. She pushed past Nikki and rushed into the living room, picking up the phone. "I'm calling my mom to come and get me," she yelled. "No way I'm staying here!"

Nikki blinked back angry tears. Martina touched her lightly on the arm. "What really happened?" she asked, keeping her voice low. "When did Alex ask Erica out?"

"When she went to the mall with my mom." Nikki choked out the words. "They ran into Alex outside the theater, and he asked her to come with him. It really wasn't my fault," Nikki insisted.

"What a mess," Martina muttered.

Haley hung up the phone and stormed back into the front hall. She looked as though she was about to cry. She yanked on her jacket and grabbed her backpack and sleeping bag.

"I guess I'd better go, too," Tori said apologetically. She gathered her things together. Haley let herself out the front door, and Tori went with her. Nikki watched through the living room window. Haley and Tori sat down on the front step to wait for Haley's mom.

"Well," Martina said, "we were right about Alex, anyway."

"Yeah," Nikki said, turning away from the window. "So why do I feel so miserable?" She flopped down on the couch.

"Maybe because you just had another big fight with one of your best friends?" Martina suggested, sitting down next to her. "Don't worry, she'll get over it."

Nikki groaned. "I don't know," she said, picking her head up. "I've never seen Haley so mad before. Not even that time at the Junior Nationals when I locked her out of our hotel room when she had that green cream all over her face." Nikki sighed. "Come to think of it, that fight was about Alex, too."

Martina smiled at her. "But look, you both got over it, didn't you?"

"Yeah," Nikki said. "But I think it's different this time. She should never have accused me of pushing Erica on Alex. I swear I didn't do that."

"I know," Martina said. "That's why I think she'll get over it. You're innocent." The girls watched through the window as a car pulled up out front and Tori and Haley got inside.

Martina stood and stretched. "Look, I think I should get going, too. Obviously there isn't going to be any party tonight. I'll call my dad."

"Okay," Nikki said. She was beginning to feel like she wanted to be alone for a while, anyway.

They talked about other things until Martina's father arrived. When Martina had gone, Nikki dragged herself upstairs to her room. She lay down on the bed and stared at the ceiling, trying not to think about Haley and Alex. Why couldn't things have stayed the same?

She heard Ben start to cry. Her mother went to get

him. A few minutes later Mrs. Simon came to Nikki's bedroom door with Ben perched on her hip. "Where is everyone?" she asked. "What was all that yelling about?"

"I had a fight with Haley. Everyone went home."

Her mother sat Ben on the bed and ran her hand through Nikki's hair, brushing it away from her face. "Are you okay? Do you want to talk about it?"

"I'm all right," Nikki answered. "I don't want to talk about it now. Maybe later."

"Okay, sweetie. Whatever it is, I'm sure you and Haley will work it out."

"Thanks, Mom," Nikki said, although she wasn't so sure.

"Are you hungry, Nikki? Do you want to eat?" Mrs. Simon asked.

Nikki shook her head, and her mother left the room. Nikki was still lying on the bed when she heard the front door slam. A minute later Erica came bouncing into the room.

"Hi!" she said, flinging herself down on the bed next to Nikki. She was beaming. "Oh, Nikki! I always thought it was hard to talk to guys, but it isn't! Alex is easy to talk to, and he's funny, and—"

"Stop it!" Nikki cried. "I don't want to hear about it."

Erica suddenly noticed Nikki's expression. "Why not? What's wrong?" she said. She glanced around the room. "And where is everybody?"

"They're not here," Nikki answered.

"But what about the sleepover?" Erica asked. "I wanted to tell Tori and Martina all about tonight."

"Erica," Nikki said, suddenly furious again, "Haley and I had a big fight. She went home, and so did everyone else. There is no sleepover, and it's all your fault."

Erica looked stunned. "My fault?" Her eyes widened. "Why is it my fault?"

"Because of the way you've been throwing yourself at Alex, that's why. Haley had a fit tonight when she heard you went to the movies with him." Nikki folded her arms. "How could you do that, anyway?"

"Why not?" Erica looked puzzled. "Why would Haley care?"

"Because she's going out with him. That's why."

"But you never told *me* that!"

"I didn't think I had to," Nikki said. "It was pretty obvious, the way Haley's been acting."

"But I even asked you about it," Erica protested. "And you said they were just friends. You did."

All the anger went out of Nikki like air out of a balloon. "You're right," she admitted. "I did say that." She punched her pillow with her fist and groaned. "I'm such an idiot sometimes. I never thought you'd be interested in Alex."

"But why didn't you just say he was going with Haley?"

"I don't know. I wasn't very happy about them going out with each other. It made me feel like such a fifth wheel." Nikki paused. "I guess I was jealous. I guess I was lying to myself, too, not just to you. I was jealous of Haley. She has everything—a great partner, tons of talent at skating, *and* a boyfriend." Nikki bit her lip.

"Hey, you're not exactly a loser," Erica said. She seemed so surprised that Nikki almost laughed.

"I feel like one," Nikki admitted. "Especially with me and Kyle sort of splitting up. And Haley doesn't have just any boyfriend—she has Alex. I mean, I know he's a great guy. He's my partner! And one of my best friends. So even if I didn't have Kyle, I had him. Someone special." Nikki paused. "I guess . . . I guess I didn't want to share him with anyone. Not even Haley."

"Poor Nikki," Erica said softly.

"I wasn't trying to keep some big secret from you," Nikki told her. "I was just confused. I didn't want to talk about it."

"I'm sorry I caused so much trouble," Erica said.

"That's okay. It wasn't your fault. I'm sorry I yelled at you. It's been a horrible night." The girls were silent for a moment. Nikki looked at the clock. It was only eight o'clock, but she was totally exhausted.

"Look," she said finally, "I think I'm going to go to bed. If you're hungry, there's chili downstairs, and my mom bought a chocolate cake."

Erica stood up. "Actually, I'm starved. Don't you want anything?"

"I can't eat. I feel too awful. What if Haley breaks up with Alex because of me?"

"Maybe it won't be so bad," Erica said. "Haley knows I'm going back to Missouri soon, so maybe she and Alex will just get back together."

"No way. You should have seen her. She was furious. She won't go out with Alex if she thinks he's interested in other girls." Nikki swallowed hard. "And she does think that—thanks to me." She put her head down on her pillow. "You know what's really weird? A few days ago, I thought this was exactly what I wanted." Tears spilled from her eyes. "I really blew it. Now Alex and Haley will break up for sure. My partner will hate me. And Haley will never be my friend again."

11

"**H**aley!" Nikki rushed across the locker room. It was Saturday morning, just before practice. Haley had taken a locker far from their usual corner.

"Look, Haley, about last night," Nikki began. "I'm sorry. I really didn't tell Erica to flirt with Alex. I—"

"Save it," Haley snapped. She sat down and yanked off a boot. "I don't want to hear it."

"But you don't know what happened," Nikki said. She had to make Haley understand.

"I said forget it!" Haley tugged at the laces on her other boot. She turned so that her back was to Nikki. "I'm not talking to you. Go away."

"So don't talk to me," Nikki said. "Just listen, okay? Erica didn't know you were going out with Alex, and—" Nikki was going to continue, but Haley

91

clapped her hands over her ears and started humming loudly.

"Great," Nikki muttered. "And you keep telling *me* to grow up." She took a step back. "All right!" she shouted at Haley. "If that's how you want to be about it, go ahead. You don't deserve an explanation!" She whirled and stalked out of the locker room.

Nikki stopped at the edge of the rink to remove her skate guards. Alex was already on the ice, warming up, but his head was down. Nikki could tell that he wasn't his usual happy self. She skated over to him and said hello.

"Hi," Alex said, barely looking up.

Nikki had never seen him so glum. "What's wrong?"

Alex raised his eyes and met Nikki's. "It's Haley," he said. "She won't even talk to me. She's acting like she's really mad," he said. "I must have done something, but what? I can't figure it out." He skated a slow circle around Nikki, looking totally miserable. "Maybe you could talk to her. She'll tell *you*. I don't know how I can fix it if I can't figure out what's wrong. Please?"

Nikki swallowed hard. She couldn't believe Alex didn't know what he'd done. And if Haley was so important to him, why had he gone out with Erica in the first place? It didn't make sense. "I already know what's wrong," she admitted.

"What? What did I do?"

"You went out on a date with Erica."

"What? I did not. What date?" Alex said.

"Last night?" Nikki said. "The movies?"

"That wasn't a date." Alex frowned. "She was just there. And it was Patrick's idea, anyway."

"Patrick?" Nikki said, puzzled. "Nobody said anything about Patrick. Erica didn't even mention him."

"He was there, all right," Alex said. "You can ask him. Or ask Erica."

"But my mom said you asked Erica if she wanted to join you."

"Maybe I did," Alex said, sounding exasperated. "Maybe I was the one who actually said, 'Hey, Erica, why don't you come to the movie?' It was Patrick's idea, though. He was probably off buying popcorn just then, but otherwise he was there the whole time. It wasn't a date. No way." He paused for a minute. "I hope you stood up for me and told Haley I wouldn't do that. I wouldn't go out with somebody else. Not now. I really like Haley—a lot."

"But how was I supposed to know that?" Nikki wailed.

"So you *didn't* stick up for me?" Alex said.

"Well, no," Nikki admitted. She blushed, thinking about how she'd been bad-mouthing Alex to Haley. "I mean, you flirt with everyone," she explained. "I didn't know you were serious about Haley. And after the way you were falling all over Erica at the mall the other day, I just thought . . ."

"Thought what?" Alex asked. "And what do you mean, falling all over Erica? I was just trying to be nice to your friend, the way you asked me to. That's what Patrick was doing, too. It's got nothing to do with how I feel about Haley."

Nikki winced. "Sorry."

"Sorry won't do me much good," Alex said. "You have to talk to Haley. You have to tell her you were wrong."

"I can't," Nikki said. "I mean, she won't listen to me. Or talk to me."

"Great," Alex said. "Thanks for ruining my life. It sure is nice to have friends." He started skating toward Kathy, who had come onto the ice and was ready for their lesson.

Nikki skated after him, hurrying to catch up. "Look, Alex, maybe I can—" she began.

"Forget it," he said furiously. "Just forget it. You've already made a mess of everything. Just stay out of it, will you?" He stopped in front of Kathy and glared at Nikki.

Kathy looked from one to the other, frowning slightly. "What's going on here?" she said finally. "Is something wrong?"

Nikki attempted to smile brightly, feeling instead as if she were baring her teeth at Kathy. "Nothing's wrong," she said.

"Yeah," Alex said. "Everything's just fine." Nobody could miss the sarcasm in his voice.

Kathy's eyebrows rose. "Well, if you won't talk about it, at least put it out of your minds for now. I don't want it to interfere with your skating. We've got a lot of work to do."

Alex stuffed his hands into the pockets of his warm-up jacket. "Right," he snapped. "You got it."

Nikki was surprised that Alex was being rude to Kathy. He must be really upset—and it was all her fault.

"All right," Kathy said. "Let's go, then."

But practice was terrible. Again.

Kathy's patience was wearing thin. "If you two don't get it together soon, you're going to embarrass yourselves at the Ice Theater performance. Not to mention me and the other members of Silver Blades. If you can't shape up, I may have to pull you out of the show." Kathy shook her head as if they were hopeless.

Nikki gulped. She didn't dare look at Alex, but she didn't have to. She could almost feel his anger, the air was so thick with tension.

She stared down at the ice. Everything was a total mess. Alex was furious with her, Kathy was disgusted with both of them, and Haley hated her. And the worst part was that it was all her fault. Her jealousy had ruined everything.

Kathy ended the practice early. Nikki dragged herself into the locker room. She was glad no one was there yet. She changed as quickly as she could and fled before she had to face Haley again.

When she got home, the only thing she wanted was to be left alone. She had just closed the door to her room when Erica bounded through the doorway, obviously excited about something.

"You won't believe it," she said. "The most incredible thing happened!"

Nikki tossed her skate bag in a corner and plopped down on her desk chair. "What?" she asked. As if she cared. As if she could care about anything except the way she'd practically ruined her whole life.

"Brandon called!" Erica said triumphantly. "He got the number from my mother and actually called me. It *was* Brandon who called the last time."

"That's nice," Nikki murmured.

"It was amazing! He said that things are really going badly and he's about to be thrown off the student council. He wants me to come home right away! He needs me to help him organize a student protest. We've got to make posters and call people, and Brandon wants me to help him write a speech. . . ." Erica hugged herself. "He said that he could never do it without me! I'm going to call the airline and see if I can get a flight home tomorrow—maybe even tonight!"

"But Erica," Nikki burst out, "you can't leave me now. You can't! My whole life is falling apart."

"You mean because Haley's mad at you?"

"Haley's mad at me, Alex is mad at me, Kathy's mad at both of us. And she's even threatening to pull us out of the Ice Theater performance." Nikki choked back a sob.

"Oh, Nikki," Erica said sympathetically. "It can't be that bad." She came to Nikki's side and hugged her.

"Yes, it can," Nikki said. "You've got to stay and help me straighten things out."

"But what can *I* do?" Erica asked.

"I don't know. Help me think of a way to get Alex and Haley back together." Nikki stood up and got a tissue from a box on her dresser, then blew her nose. "Anyway, it's partly your fault for flirting with Alex like that. And you never even told me Patrick was at the movies, too," she said accusingly.

"Oh, yeah, he was," Erica said.

"But I thought you were on a real date with Alex. That's what I told Haley, and now she's not speaking to him, so he's mad at me, too. And then Alex said it wasn't a date at all."

"It wasn't, I guess," Erica said. She looked a little embarrassed. "But it was fun to flirt with him. I guess I got carried away."

"Well, that's Alex," Nikki said. "He *is* fun to be with. The trouble is, he can be hard to resist. But he didn't mean anything by it." She wadded up the tissue and threw it in the garbage. "But you will stay and help me, won't you? Please?"

"Well . . ." Erica hesitated. "I really do owe you— I've found a whole new side of myself since I've been here." She smiled. "Okay. I guess Brandon can handle things by himself for a little longer. Besides, what are old friends for?"

"Thanks. I really, really appreciate it," Nikki said.

"I know." Erica sat cross-legged on the bed. "Now come on," she said. "Let's stop worrying about what went wrong and come up with a plan. Something that will get your two lovebirds back together again. And fast!"

12

Nikki took a deep breath and picked up the phone. Her heart was pounding, and her hand trembled slightly. She felt as nervous as she did before a big competition. Maybe even more nervous.

"Go on," Erica urged. "You can do it. You *have* to do it."

"I know." Nikki read the number out of her address book. It was Sunday, Kathy's day off. But Kathy had given all her students her home number in case of an emergency. And as far as Nikki was concerned, this *was* an emergency.

"Hello?"

"Uh, Kathy, hi. It's me, Nikki." Even her voice was shaky.

"Oh. Hello, Nikki. What's up?" Kathy asked.

Nikki hesitated, thinking about how Kathy had

threatened to pull them out of the Ice Theater show.
"I—I—" Nikki stammered. She took a deep breath. "I
need to ask you a favor."

"What is it?" Kathy asked.

"Well, Alex is mad at me," Nikki explained. "Really
mad at me. I kind of messed things up between him
and Haley. That's the reason we started having so
much trouble skating together. I was upset that they
were going out with each other. And then I sort of
accidentally got Haley mad at Alex, and now he's mad
at me." Nikki wished her voice wouldn't shake. "So I
have to do something to get them back together again.
If I don't, Alex will be mad at me forever, and we'll
never be able to skate well together again."

"Oh, Nikki." Kathy sighed. "I've told you to keep
your personal life and your skating separate."

"I know," Nikki said. "And I've been trying, really I
have. But it's so hard. If you'll help me just this once, I
promise it won't happen again. I've learned my lesson,
honest."

"Good," Kathy said. "I'm sincerely glad to hear
that." She paused. "I don't see how I can help you,
though."

"I need you to get Alex to the rink. Could you call
him and tell him that you want to work with him alone
this afternoon, after the public session?"

"I'm not in the habit of lying to my students," Kathy
said.

Nikki squirmed. Sarge sure wasn't making this any
easier. "I know," Nikki said. "And I wouldn't ask you

if I could think of another way. Really, I wouldn't. But I can't. And if I don't do something fast, Alex and I will never be ready for the Ice Theater show."

There was a long pause. Nikki held her breath, waiting for Kathy to reply.

Finally Kathy sighed. "Okay," she said. "I'll do it. What time do you want him there?"

Nikki exhaled in relief. "Three-forty-five. Thanks, Kathy."

"You're welcome. And Nikki?"

"Yes?"

"I won't do something like this again, do you understand?"

"Yes." In spite of Kathy's warning, Nikki smiled broadly. It was going to work. It had to work.

"Okay. I'll call him now. Unless there's a problem, I won't call you back."

"Okay."

They said good-bye and hung up. "Whew," Nikki said. She suddenly realized how hard she'd been gripping the receiver. "One down, one to go," she told Erica.

She picked up the phone and dialed again.

"Patrick should be easier, at least," Erica said.

"He couldn't be much harder, that's for sure."

When Nikki got Patrick on the phone, she explained that she was trying to get Haley and Alex back together again.

"Good," Patrick said. "Haley was miserable yesterday."

"I know," Nikki said, feeling guilty. "So was Alex."

"So what do you want me to do?"

"Just call Haley and tell her to come to the rink at four o'clock. Tell her you have a special surprise for her or something. It doesn't matter what. Just make sure she goes."

"Sure," Patrick said. "I can manage that."

"Great," Nikki said. "Thanks. I owe you one. Big-time."

"I'll remember that," Patrick said.

"This is it," Erica said. "It's almost three-forty-five." They were standing by the bleachers at the rink. The public session had ended at three-thirty, and Mack was grooming the ice with the huge Zamboni.

"I can't believe how nervous I am," Nikki said. She held out her hand. "Look, I'm actually shaking. What if this doesn't work?"

"It will," Erica said. "It has to, right?"

"Right," Nikki agreed. "Because if it doesn't, Haley and Alex will never speak to me again. Not that it will matter, because I'll be dead. Kathy will kill me."

"Look," Erica said suddenly, pointing to the doors leading to the ice. "There he is. There's Alex."

Nikki pulled Erica back so that they were hidden from Alex's view. She didn't want him to see them until he was right next to them. He might turn around and leave at the sight of her. Alex walked in their direction, toward the locker room. "Alex," Nikki said when he was just a few feet away. She and Erica stepped away from the bleachers.

Alex almost jumped. "What are you two doing here?" he asked coldly. "Kathy said she wanted to work with me alone."

"Well, actually," Nikki began, "Kathy isn't here."

"But she told me to meet her at three-forty-five." Alex looked puzzled.

"I know. I asked her to. I just had to talk to you."

"Oh, great," he said. "Now you've got Kathy lying for you. You're really something, Nikki." He turned and started to walk away. "Whatever it is you've got to tell me, I don't want to hear it. So just forget it."

"Wait, Alex, please," Nikki said, hustling to keep up with him. "Stay. Just for a minute."

"You won't be sorry," Erica added. "We just want to explain." He kept walking.

"Kathy's going to pull us out of the show if we don't work this out," Nikki said desperately.

Alex slowed, then stopped. Nikki breathed a sigh of relief. "Thanks," she said. "You won't be sorry."

"This had better be good," Alex grumbled, crossing his arms. "Really good."

"First of all," Nikki said, "I'm very sorry for interfering with things between you and Haley. I guess . . . no, I *know* I was jealous." She dropped her eyes. "I felt like if you guys got together, you wouldn't need me anymore." Nikki raised her eyes and looked Alex in the face. "I don't know . . . I felt like I was losing my two best friends at once. I kind of went crazy, I guess."

"Uh-huh," Alex said. He still looked as though he was waiting for her to prove something to him, but his expression had softened.

"And then," Erica piped up, "I came along. Nikki kind of, uh, forgot to mention that you were going out with Haley. And you were so nice to me that I guess I got a little carried away."

"It wasn't Erica's fault," Nikki put in.

"Well, I don't usually get much attention from guys," Erica admitted, blushing. "I took it the wrong way. I didn't even tell Nikki that Patrick was at the movies with us. I kind of wanted to pretend it was a real date." She turned even redder, and Alex started to smile.

"Well," Alex said, "it's a well-known fact that I am pretty irresistible." He unfolded his arms and stuck his hands in his jacket pockets.

Nikki's mouth dropped open. "See? You can't help it!" she said. "You live to flirt! Admit it, Alex—Erica wasn't totally crazy."

"Okay," Alex said, "I admit it. I can't help it. Girls just have that effect on me."

Nikki groaned. "There you go again."

"But," Alex added, "I really do like Haley a different way."

Nikki looked over at the rink entrance. "Yikes!" she cried. "Could you tell her that, then? Quick."

Haley stood just inside the door. She was staring hard at the three of them.

"Haley, wait!" Alex called. But Haley whirled around and headed out the door.

"Wait, Haley!" Nikki shouted. She sprinted after her.

Erica joined the chase. "Haley, please, I need to tell you something important. Please. It's not what you think."

Haley pushed through the doors to the lobby but then hesitated. She finally stopped. Nikki and Erica caught up with her. "I've got to talk to you," Erica said. "That's why Nikki asked Patrick to get you here."

"He said he had a surprise for me," Haley said. "I thought he was trying to cheer me up. I didn't realize it was going to be a nasty surprise," she said, looking straight at Nikki.

Erica cleared her throat. "Listen, about Alex," she said. "There was nothing between us. I was sort of practicing on him—flirting with him and acting like we were on a date at the movies. But we weren't. I mean, Patrick was there, too."

Haley's eyes widened in surprise. "Why didn't you tell me that?" she asked Nikki. "Didn't you think it was important?"

"I didn't know!" Nikki burst out. "Not at first. And by the time I found out, you wouldn't listen to a word I said."

"Anyway," Erica said, "I wanted to tell you that I'm

not interested in Alex. There's this guy back home I really like. So you shouldn't be mad at Alex or me. Honest."

"Really?" Haley still seemed angry, but there was a hint of relief in her voice, too. She looked from Erica to the glass doors. Alex was still there, watching her. Haley turned back to Erica.

"Really," Erica assured her.

"Thanks for telling me, Erica. It's nice to know somebody cares about my feelings around here." She continued talking to Erica as if Nikki weren't even there. "You can tell your friend, though, that I'm still mad at her." Haley peered through the glass doors again. "I've got to go. There's someone else I want to talk to." She pushed through the doors, leaving them behind.

"Whew," Nikki said. She slumped onto a bench in the lobby. "Do you think it worked?"

Erica looked through the doors at Haley and Alex. "They're smiling at each other," she reported. "And she's sort of, um, glowing. It's definitely okay," she said, and sat down. "Haley is still mad at you, though," she pointed out.

"I know. But as soon as she and Alex are back together, she'll get happy again. Then she'll forgive me. I hope." Nikki glanced up at the clock on the lobby wall. "Yikes!" she said, jumping up. "We'd better call my mom and get home, or you're going to miss your plane!"

Erica bolted off the bench. "Uh-oh," she said.

"You're right. Let's go. If I miss that plane, we'll both be in trouble!"

Nikki groaned and held up her hands. "No, please," she said. "I can't take having any more people mad at me." She walked over to the pay phone and dropped in a quarter. "You know," she said, "there's one thing you have to admit about this vacation."

"What's that?" Erica asked.

"Neither of us will *ever* forget it."

"Boy," Erica said, "you sure got that right."

13

Nikki opened a locker in the Ice Theater of Philadelphia dressing room. She set down her skate bag, then hung up her Silver Blades warm-up jacket and skating dress. She looked around. This was it at last.

It was early, and the locker room was nearly empty. Nikki had been worried that they might get caught in traffic and be late. She had made her parents leave long before they really needed to.

She wasn't the only early bird, though. Across the room she saw Karen Morris, the skating star, slipping into a sparkly red skating dress. Her long brown hair was tied up in a bun fastened with a red ribbon. She looked even prettier than she did on television. Nikki watched her struggle to fasten the back of her dress. Wow, she thought, she's just a regular person, like anyone else.

Nikki had to ask for Karen's autograph. This might be her only chance! She grabbed a pen and a picture of Karen and Michael. She had carefully ripped it out of *Skating* magazine.

Nikki's heart was pounding as she crossed the locker room and approached Karen. "Excuse me," she said, holding out the pen and picture, "but would you mind . . ."

Karen looked up and smiled. "Of course not," she said. "I'll sign that if you'll help me with this stupid hook and eye." She gave up fiddling with the dress and took the pen and picture. "What's your name?" she asked.

"Nikki. Nikki Simon. My partner and I are skating in the show today."

Karen scribbled on the picture and handed it back to Nikki. "That's great," she said. "I hope you're not as nervous as I am. Right now I can't even get my fingers to work right. Here," she said, turning around. "Can you get this?"

Nikki fastened the hook and eye. "You're nervous?" she asked.

"Petrified," Karen admitted. "It happens every time. Once I step onto the ice I'm okay, but beforehand I'm a total wreck. You'd think I'd be over it by now, but I'm not."

"I'm nervous, too," Nikki admitted. "But I'd never guess that you were. You always look so cool when you perform. I watch you on TV whenever I can," she added. "You and Michael are my favorite skaters."

"Thank you," Karen said. She pulled a pair of skates out of her locker. "Good luck out there today."

"Thanks," Nikki said. Other skaters were starting to arrive, and a young woman Nikki didn't recognize greeted Karen. Nikki said good-bye and walked back to her locker. She carefully tucked the picture back into her bag and then pulled out her skates.

Something huge, black, and hairy came with them. A spider!

It bounced onto the locker room floor and lay still.

Nikki shook her head. She knew instantly that it wasn't real. The fake spider trick was *very* familiar. She glanced around suspiciously.

"Gotcha!" Haley popped out from behind a locker, her brown eyes sparkling.

"Haley! You creep!" Nikki yelled, but she was smiling. "What are you doing here?" she asked. "I thought you were still mad at me."

Haley plopped down on the bench. "Naw," she said. "I decided to forgive you."

"Finally," Nikki said. "I thought you were going to stay mad at me forever. It's been a whole week."

"I know," Haley said. "A whole week of avoiding each other in the locker room." She suddenly got very serious. "I finally realized something last night."

"What?"

"I missed you. Really, really missed you. And suddenly it seemed stupid, not being friends anymore." She looked up at Nikki. "What do you think?" she asked. "Can we just forget all that stuff that happened and be friends again?"

"Yes!" Nikki cried. "I tried to tell you how sorry I was, but you wouldn't listen." Haley started to say something, but Nikki wouldn't let her. "I really am sorry," she went on, "about the things I said about Alex." She lowered her voice. "I was jealous. I was afraid that if you and Alex got together, I'd lose you both. If you had each other, why would you need me?"

Haley looked surprised. She jumped up and hugged Nikki. "Are you kidding? Not need you? I need all the friends I can get, Alex or no Alex. Especially friends like you. Besides, when have boyfriends ever been able to take the place of girlfriends?"

Nikki swallowed the lump that had suddenly risen in her throat. She hugged Haley back. "Never," she said. "Not in my book, anyway."

Haley hugged her again. "Good," she said. "Now you'd better get changed. Unless you expect to skate in those." She pointed to Nikki's jeans.

"Right," Nikki said. She slipped off her shoes and unzipped her jeans. "I am so nervous," she confided.

"You'll be fine," Haley assured her.

"Promise?"

"Promise."

Nikki started dressing, and then she remembered something. "There's a letter from Erica in my bag," she said. "You should read it. It's in the pocket, on the outside."

Haley reached in and pulled out an envelope. She unfolded the letter and read it aloud.

Dear Nikki,

I hope this letter reaches you before your performance at the Ice Theater. Believe me, I will be thinking of you on Sunday. I hope it goes great!

I'm so glad I got to come visit and meet all your friends. They're terrific. I will never forget everything they did for me. Nobody here can believe how great I look! My dad actually did a double take when I got off the plane. It was so funny!

We managed to save Brandon's job as student council president—but just barely. He didn't have to apologize. But he can't write any more articles for the paper about teachers or school policies. Freedom of speech is dead and buried at Mapleview Junior High! It stinks, but to tell you the truth, I've been too happy the last few days to care much!

That's because Brandon's been paying a lot more attention to me—or maybe I should say a different kind of attention. He actually flirts with me. And I flirt back, too—like mad! I think he's going to ask me out any day now. I can't wait!

Good luck with your performance. I know you and Alex will steal the show!

Love,
Erica

"That's great about Brandon," Haley said, folding the letter back up. "I hope it works out for her."

"Me too," Nikki said. "And I hope she's right about us stealing the show. I'm afraid we might ruin it instead."

"Hey, I told you, you'll be fine," Haley said.

"Well, I am *really* nervous," Nikki said, putting on her skates. "But actually, I think you're right. Alex and I have been working so hard since Erica left. You know all the extra practice time we've been putting in. And then the other day everything just sort of clicked." She paused. "When it works, when Alex and I skate well, it's like no other feeling in the world."

Nikki slipped her arms into the sleeves of her skating dress. She turned around, and Haley zipped her up.

"I know," Haley said. "It's the same for me and Patrick. It's like magic."

"Yeah." Nikki put on her warm-up jacket. "Well," she said, "time to go warm up." The locker room was bustling with activity, and she knew the ice would be crowded soon. "Alex is probably waiting for me," she added.

"Okay," Haley said. "I'll see you later."

Nikki started to leave, then turned back to Haley. "Thanks for coming," she said. "It really means a lot to me."

Haley smiled. "I wouldn't have missed it for the world."

Forty-five minutes later Nikki and Alex stood by the boards, waiting for their turn to skate. The butterflies in Nikki's stomach were doing spins and jumps of their own.

"And now," Nikki heard the announcer say, "please give a warm welcome to a young pair from Seneca Hills, Pennyslvania, Nikki Simon and Alex Beekman."

Alex took Nikki's hand, and they stepped onto the ice. The crowd clapped wildly. Nikki's heart pounded as she and Alex skated to center ice. They struck their opening pose. Their music from *Grease* began, and the crowd seemed to fade away. Nikki focused completely on the routine—and on Alex.

They performed flawlessly. When they reached the throw double axel, Alex lifted Nikki into the air and propelled her into two and a half perfect rotations. Nikki landed solidly on one foot, her arms fully extended.

A huge smile spread across Nikki's face. From the corner of her eye she could see Alex smiling, too. They finished their routine with a flourish, then took their bows and left the ice. The audience's applause followed them.

Haley was right, Nikki thought as she and Alex skated to the edge of the ice. At times like this, skating with Alex really was magic.

As they stepped off the ice, Haley was waiting for them.

"That was incredible," she said. She wrapped Nikki in a big hug. Nikki hugged her back.

"Hey, what about me?" Alex demanded.

Haley grinned. She gave Alex a huge hug. Alex kissed Haley on the tip of her nose.

Nikki beamed at them. It's all right, she thought. I'm glad they're together. And finally, she really, truly was.

school, has a plan that's sure to get her into *big* trouble. Could this be the end of Jill's skating career?

#5: The Perfect Pair

Nikki Simon and Alex Beekman are the perfect pair on the ice. But off the ice there's a big problem. Suddenly Alex is sending Nikki gifts and asking her out on dates. Nikki wants to be Alex's partner in pairs but not his girlfriend. Will she lose Alex when she tells him? Can Nikki's friends in Silver Blades find a way to save her friendship with Alex *and* her skating career?

#6: Skating Camp

Summer's here and Jill can't wait to join her best friends from Silver Blades at skating camp. It's going to be just like old times. But things have changed since Jill left Silver Blades to train at a famous ice academy. Tori and Danielle are spending all their time with another skater, Haley Arthur, and Nikki has a big secret that she won't share with anyone. Has Jill lost her best friends forever?

#7: The Ice Princess

Tori's favorite skating superstar, Elyse Taylor, is in town, and she's staying with Tori! When Elyse promises to teach Tori her famous spin, Tori's sure they'll become the best of friends. But Elyse isn't the sweet champion everyone thinks she is. And she's going to make problems for Tori!

#8: Rumors at the Rink

Haley can't believe it—Kathy Bart, her favorite coach in the whole world, is quitting Silver Blades! Haley's sure it's all her fault. Why didn't she listen when everyone told her to stop playing practical jokes on Kathy? With Kathy gone, Haley knows she'll never win the next big competition. She has to make Kathy change her mind—no matter what. But will Haley's secret plan work?

#9: Spring Break

Jill is home from the Ice Academy, and everyone is treating her like a star. And she loves it! It's like a dream come true—especially when she meets cute, fifteen-year-old Ryan McKensey. He's so fun and cool—and he happens to be her number-one fan! The only problem is that he doesn't understand what it takes to be a professional athlete. Jill doesn't want to ruin her chances with such a great guy. But will dating Ryan destroy her future as an Olympic skater?

#10: Center Ice

It's gold medal time for Tori—she just knows it! The next big competition is coming up, and Tori has a winning routine. Now all she needs is that fabulous skating dress her mother promised her! But Mrs. Carsen doesn't seem to be interested in Tori's skating anymore—not since she started dating a new man in town. When Mrs. Carsen tells Tori she's not going to the competition, Tori decides enough is enough! She has a plan that will change everything—forever!

#11: A Surprise Twist

Danielle's on top of the world! All her hard work at the rink has paid off. She's good. Very good. And Dani's new English teacher, Ms. Howard, says she has a real flair for writing—she might even be the best writer in her class. Trouble is, there's a big skating competition coming up—*and* a writing contest. Dani's stumped. Her friends and family are counting on her to skate her best. But Ms. Howard is counting on her to write a winning story. How can Dani choose between skating and her new passion?

#12: The Winning Spirit

A group of Special Olympic skaters is on the way to Seneca Hills! The skaters are going to pair up with the Silver Blades members in a mini-competition. Everyone in Silver Blades thinks Nikki Simon is really lucky—her Special Olympics partner is Carrie, a girl with Down syndrome who's one of the best visiting skaters. But Nikki can't seem to warm up to the idea of skating with Carrie. In fact, she seems to be hiding something . . . but what?

#13: The Big Audition

Holiday excitement is in the air! Jill Wong, one of Silver Blades' best skaters, is certain she will win the leading role of Clara in the *Nutcracker on Ice* spectacular. Until young skater Amber Armstrong comes along. At first Jill can't believe that Amber is serious competition. But she had better believe it— and fast! Because she's about to find herself completely out of the spotlight.

#14: Nutcracker on Ice

Nothing is going Jill Wong's way. She hates her role in the *Nutcracker on Ice* spectacular. And she's hardly on the ice long enough to be noticed! To top it all off, the Ice Academy coaches seem awfully impressed with Jill's main rival, Amber Armstrong. Jill has worked so hard to return to the Academy, and now she might lose her chance. Does Jill have what it takes to save her lifelong dream?

Super Edition #1: Rinkside Romance

Tori, Haley, Nikki, and Amber are at the Junior Nationals, where a figure skater's dreams can really come true! But Amber's trying too hard, and her skating is awful. Tori's in trouble with an important judge. Nikki and Alex are fighting so much they might not make it into the competition. And someone is sending them all mysterious love notes! Are their skating dreams about to turn into nightmares?

#15: A New Move

Haley's got a big problem. Lately her parents have been fighting more than ever. And now her dad is moving out—and going to live in Canada! Haley just doesn't see how she can live without him. Especially since the only thing her mom and sister ever talk about is her sister's riding. They don't care about Haley's skating at all! There's one clever move that could solve all Haley's problems. Does she have the nerve to go through with it?

#16: Ice Magic

Martina Nemo has always dreamed of skating in the Ice Capades. So when she lands a skating role in a television movie, it seems too good to be true! Martina loves to perform in front of the camera. It's a lot of fun—especially when all her friends in Silver Blades visit her on the set to cheer her on. Then Martina discovers something terrible: Someone is out to ruin her chance of a lifetime. . . .

#17: A Leap Ahead

Amber Armstrong is only eleven, but she can already skate as well as—even better than—the older girls in Silver Blades. The only problem is that the other skaters still treat her like a baby. So Amber decides to take the senior-level skating test. She'll be the youngest skater ever to pass, and then the other girls will *have* to stop treating her like a little kid. Amber is sure her plan will work. But is she headed for success or for total disaster?

DO YOU HAVE A YOUNGER BROTHER OR SISTER?

Maybe he or she would like to meet Jill Wong's little sister Randi and her friends in the exciting new series

SILVER BLADES™

FIGURE EIGHTS

Look for these titles at your bookstore or library:

ICE DREAMS
STAR FOR A DAY
THE BEST ICE SHOW EVER!
BOSSY ANNA
DOUBLE BIRTHDAY TROUBLE

and coming soon:
SPECIAL DELIVERY MESS

LEARN TO SKATE!

SKATE WITH U.S.
A SPECIAL PROGRAM FOR BEGINNERS

WHAT IS **SKATE WITH U.S.?**

Designed by the United States Figure Skating Association (USFSA) and sponsored by the United States Postal Service, Skate With U.S. is a beginning ice-skating program that is fun, challenging, and rewarding. Skaters of all ages are welcome!

HOW DO I JOIN **SKATE WITH U.S.?**

Skate With U.S. is offered at many rinks and clubs across the country. Contact your local rink or club to see if it offers the USFSA Basic Skills program. Or **call 1-800-269-0166** for more information about the Skate With U.S. program in your area.

WHAT DO I GET WHEN I JOIN **SKATE WITH U.S.?**

When you join Skate With U.S. through a club or a rink, you will be registered as an official USFSA Basic Skills Member, and you will receive:

- Official Basic Skills Membership Card
- Basic Skills Record Book with stickers
- Official Basic Skills member patch
- Year patch, denoting membership year
  And much, much more!

PLUS you may be eligible to participate in a "Compete With U.S." competition hosted by sponsoring clubs and rinks!

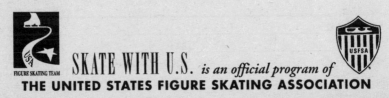

SKATE WITH U.S. *is an official program of*
THE UNITED STATES FIGURE SKATING ASSOCIATION

A FAN CLUB—JUST FOR YOU!

JOIN THE USA FIGURE SKATING INSIDE TICKET FAN CLUB!

As a member of this special skating fan club, you get:

- **Six issues of SKATING MAGAZINE!**
  For the inside edge on what's happening on and off the ice!

- **Your very own copy of MAGIC MEMORIES ON ICE!**
  A 90-minute video produced by ABC Sports featuring the world's greatest skaters!

- **An Official USA FIGURE SKATING TEAM Pin!**
  Available only to Inside Ticket Fan Club members!

- **A limited-edition photo of the U.S. World Figure Skating Team!**
  Available only to Inside Ticket Fan Club members!

- **The Official USA FIGURE SKATING INSIDE TICKET Membership Card!** For special discounts on USA Figure Skating collectibles and memorabilia!

To join the USA FIGURE SKATING INSIDE TICKET Fan Club, fill out the form below and send it with $24.95, plus $3.95 for shipping and handling (U.S. funds only, please!), to:

> Sports Fan Network
> USA Figure Skating Inside Ticket
> P.O. Box 581
> Portland, Oregon 97207-0581

Or call the Sports Fan Network membership hotline at **1-800-363-8796!**

NAME:_____

ADDRESS:_____

CITY:_____**STATE:**_____**ZIP:**_____

PHONE: (___)_____**DATE OF BIRTH:**_____